PU[FFIN]

A[...]

The tiny island off Scotla[nd...]
seemed an ideal place for [...]
to take a break from the p[...]

But lying innocently on [...]
A little boy called Pog found it. His older sister Mee and her
friend discovered its remarkable powers – powers which led
them into a nightmare experience on a submarine as they
tried desperately to keep the pebble out of enemy hands.

Nicholas Fisk's very readable novel of adventure and possibility (it's almost but not entirely a science fiction story) is
set firmly in the modern world of political intrigue, and it
will be enjoyed particularly by 9- to 11-year olds.

ANTIGRAV

NICHOLAS FISK

PUFFIN BOOKS

Puffin Books, Penguin Books Ltd, Harmondsworth, Middlesex, England
Penguin Books, 625 Madison Avenue, New York, New York 10022, U.S.A.
Penguin Books Australia Ltd, Ringwood, Victoria, Australia
Penguin Books Canada Ltd, 2801 John Street, Markham, Ontario, Canada L3R 1B4
Penguin Books (N.Z.) Ltd, 182-190 Wairau Road, Auckland 10, New Zealand

—

First published by Kestrel Books 1978
Published in Puffin Books 1982

—

Copyright © Nicholas Fisk 1978
All rights reserved

—

Reproduced, printed and bound in Great Britain by
Cox & Wyman Ltd, Reading

Except in the United States of America,
this book is sold subject to the condition
that it shall not, by way of trade or otherwise,
be lent, re-sold, hired out, or otherwise circulated
without the publisher's prior consent in any form of
binding or cover other than that in which it is
published and without a similar condition
including this condition being imposed
on the subsequent purchaser

Train, Mee and Pog squatted on the stony shore. The sea was only yards away. They were overhung by a great black rock and most of the stones on the shore were black too. Others were brown, ochre, grey, marbled – the usual stones.

Mee said, 'Here's another special! Black with gold flecks! Look, Pog!' She showed the stone to her three-year-old brother, Pog. He took it carefully in his fat hand. Pleased, he said, 'Special. Oh yes. In the tube?' She said, 'Fine. Put it with the others.' So Pog picked up the Smarties tube and added the new stone to the others. The tube was nearly filled with black and gold stones.

'Red stone now?' Pog said. '*My* stone?'

'Just one more black and gold, Pog,' Train said. 'See if you can find it yourself. Then we'll put your red stone in, and put the cap on, and that will be that. All complete!'

''Plete,' Pog said. He began to search for the last black and gold stone. Mee winked at Train: he smiled back and whispered, 'He likes being busy!'

Pog picked up stones, looked at them, threw them away. 'Not you,' he said. 'Go away.'

Very soon he found the stone he wanted and brought it to Train and Mee. Mee said, 'Not too big . . . Not too small . . . Just right! So we'll pop it in with the others – like – *this*!'

'Poppy tin,' Pog said. 'Oh yes.' The stone went *click*. The tube was almost full. 'Now my stone,' said Pog. 'My red stone!' He kept his red stone in the pocket of his red bathing trunks. He constantly checked that it was there, safe and sound. It was his stone, the red stone, the magic stone. The only red stone on the island.

'There!' he said, holding out the red stone. 'Red!' It was only a pebble really. But it was certainly red. As red as his trunks. A glowing red.

'Shall I put it in for you, Pog?' said Train, standing up and stretching. He looked very tall against Pog and Mee wondered what Pog would be like when he was twelve, like Train.

'No. Pog do it.' He put the Smarties tube firmly into Mee's right hand and placed the plastic cap of the tube in her left hand. Everything had to be just right before he dropped his red stone in the tube.

'I hereby declare Pog's collection complete!' said Train. ''Plete!' echoed Pog and dropped the red pebble. 'I hereby crown thee and name thee Pog's Collection!' said Mee as she put the plastic cap on the tube. Her right hand held the tube, her left hand was over the cap–

And then it happened. 'It's pulling!' she cried. 'Lifting!' Train laughed, but stopped laughing: Mee's face was strange, her eyes were popping, her mouth was open with shock. The muscles of her arms were showing–

'Help me!' she said. 'Hang on to it! It's lifting like mad!'

Train put his hands over hers. She cried, 'No! One hand on the cap! It will fly off if you don't!'

Train obeyed, wondering if it was all some kind of joke. For a second, Mee relaxed and Train knew it was no joke. He felt the tube thrust upwards against his strength, as if it were a rocket trying to take off.

'This is impossible!' he said. 'It can't possibly be – '

'Just hang on!' Mee said. 'Hang on, that's all!'

*

Two days earlier . . .

It was all talk, laughter and bustle and 'Give us a hand with this!' on the seashore, but Mee felt lonely and self-conscious. She could tell her mother felt the same way. Her mother's face was fixed in a set half-smile, the sort of smile that makes your jaw ache after half an hour or so.

'All right, Amelia?' her mother said.

'Oh, yes!' Mee replied, making her voice enthusiastic. She thought, 'That proves she's nervous. She never calls me "Amelia" unless she's cross or nervous . . .'

'It's a gorgeous place, isn't it?' her mother said, brightly. The name of the place was Tarantay Ear. It was a small island to the north-west of Scotland. In the clear, slanting, golden light of early evening it was very beautiful – a black, green and gold castle amid blue lawns, which were the sea. The sea itself was a deep, living blue, sparkled by distant white horses that appeared and disappeared like conjuring tricks. Over there, gleaming in the low sun, Mee saw the neighbouring island. Its name was Luish. It was smaller than Tarantay Ear. There were a dozen more or less habitable cottages on Tarantay, but none on Luish.

'Gorgeous!' Mee said, trying to convince herself that she was sharing the emotions the others seemed to be feeling. They were all scientists. Most of them were behaving like children let out of school. There was no one of her own age, though Mee and her mother had been told that the next boat might bring one or two children as well as more scientists. The boats were so small that they could only carry twelve people at a time. The second dozen would complete the party.

'Look at him!' her mother said, nodding her head at Pog. He was holding up a little red stone. 'Red!' he said, proudly. He looked so pleased and fat-stomached that Mee genuinely smiled.

Doctor Leo Alexander came down on them like a hawk and spoiled the pleasure. He turned to Mee and said, 'I nearly said "Dear Mee", but of course, that comes out all wrong, doesn't it? But I can say "Dear Amelia" can't I? And give you an uncley sort of kiss?' He kissed Mee and she felt her face go red with annoyance. He was being Good to her and her mother again – including them in the party, making sure they didn't feel left out of things. He had been doing this ever since Father died. He had got Mother her job as secretary of S.I.I., the Science International Institute; got them their place on the Institute's holiday fortnight on the island ('It will mean everything to the children, Peg. And a lot . . . to me . . .!') and got much too close for comfort to things that Mee wanted kept at a distance. But her mother was still smiling.

Now Leo was pointing at Pog and saying, self-mockingly, 'Here am I, Peg, *eminent* physicist, *noted* geologist, *affable* TV personality, put to shame by a young person named Pog!'

Mee's mother said, 'What's Pog done to put you to shame, Leo?'

'Well, look at the pebbles on the beach! Regard them closely! *Peer* at them! Can you see a single *red* pebble anywhere, Peg? Can you, Mee? Look! Really look!'

They looked, really looked. Leo Alexander was, as usual, right. No red pebbles. 'But Pog found a red pebble!' said Leo. 'Probably the only red pebble within a hundred miles! Can I look at it, Pog?'

'No.'

'Oh, go on, Pog, be a sport.' Leo took the pebble and examined it carefully. He muttered a lot of scientific words that Mee did not understand. Pog said 'Mine now' and stretched out his hand. Leo gave the pebble back. Pog put it in his pocket, and ran away. Watching him run – fall down – pick himself up – fall down – run again, Mee felt happy again. 'He doesn't even notice the falls,' she thought. 'He just gets up and goes on , like a little tank.' She thought about this as she watched her baby brother. 'You're always thinking about yourself,' she told herself. 'Pog doesn't think about himself, he just ploughs on. But then, he doesn't even know he *is* himself yet. Or that his name is Timothy, not Pog – and I'm his sister – and he hasn't got a father – '

She switched off her thoughts at this point and studied the people on the beach. An international group. Most of them had got their rucksacks and tents and other things on their shoulders. Some were struggling up the steep hill, making for the deserted cottages or looking about for tent sites. There was a lot of shouting and laughter. A weedy man with very white legs and black ankle socks was pushing the knapsack of a young woman wearing jeans and a bright red shirt. The young woman was almost beautiful in a soft, foreign-looking way. Her dark hair was swept back into a topknot. Her hair was almost straight, but frizzy near her temples and on the nape of her neck. She had high cheekbones. Another man came to join the weedy man and the girl turned round, smiling, to say 'No, I do not need'. 'Foreign,' thought Mee. 'I was right. She looks nice.'

The low sun seemed to set the red shirt on fire and Mee looked at it through half-closed eyes, thinking about nothing. Then her mother touched her arm and said 'Look!'

Glittering on the sea was the other fishing boat, bringing the other half of the island party.

*

On the other fishing boat, Train tried to keep his attention fixed on the island, but couldn't. His eyes kept slipping back to the amazing bald head of the man sitting below him (Train was standing) in the bows of the boat. Train had never seen a totally bald man before. He had seen men with very little hair, or no hair worth speaking of, but this man was different. His skull almost seemed to have a balloon above it with the word BALD! written on it and a red and yellow arrow pointing to his scalp. 'No one', Train thought to himself, 'can be that bald.'

Train looked at the island again, but his mind went on thinking about the bald man, and the way the sun made polished highlights on his skull, and the thickness of his lips, and the heaviness of the folds on either side of his nose. The folds covered in the corners of his mouth, giving him a sulky, glowering look. The man wore elaborate sandals of reddish leather, cream socks, slate-grey trousers and a cream knitted sports shirt with short sleeves and elaborate patterns woven into the material in vertical bands. A bright blue anorak was slung over his massive, sloping shoulders. He wore a big chromium-plated wristwatch on his left wrist. The wrist, thought Train, must be as thick as my Sunday-best biceps; and his biceps look about twice the thickness of my thighs.

The man moved. He swung his head, slowly, to look at the island. There were two and a half creases in his bull neck. They rolled over each other oilily as his neck turned. He glared palely at the island for a few seconds, then swung his head back again. The creases sorted themselves out smoothly into their former pattern.

Train said to himself, 'Go on, be a hero! Say something to him!' Aloud, he said, 'That's it! That's our island!'

The man lifted and turned his head. The action seemed to take many seconds. His eyes at last met Train's eyes and Train thought, 'Last one in's a cissy!' – for meeting the man's eyes was just like jumping into a swimming pool on an icy morning.

'Our island!' repeated Train, bravely.

'The island,' said the man in a surprisingly high, light, hoarse tenor. 'So.' The conversation was Train said, 'Yes, that's the island all right!' and felt feeble. So he stared fixedly at the island, willing himself to pick out details.

The island was even smaller than he thought it would be. He had not expected any grass, but there was some. The water would be cold, but there might be good snorkelling around those black rocks where the waves were breaking. He saw little figures carrying bundles moving up the steep sides and wondered where his father and he would pitch their tent. Probably very high, his father liked big views – which was strange for a man who spent his working life peering at stones and hitting them with a special little hammer.

He saw a few people on the beach. A tiny little figure with copper hair, almost a baby. A woman with the same colour hair: must be the mother. And another woman. Or was it a girl? A girl, definitely. Train was glad. There were two boys and one girl on his boat. They kept shouting TV catchphrases at each other and yelling with laughter. The girl on the beach might be more interesting.

As he examined the island, he forgot about the bald man and thought, 'What a smashing place. Two weeks of it, with the sea, and snorkelling, and living in a tent!' He thought about the things he and his father would do. His father would work a lot, of course. He always did, work was his drug. But he would not work all the time. There would be the usual curry-making sessions – the knapsacks bulged with spices and dishes and tins. There would be his father's small, almost secretive jokes that amused Train more than any other jokes – jokes that made his father laugh, apparently unwillingly. He would come snorkelling even if the water was freezing, because he would not admit to Train or anyone else that it was cold. If Train started something – building a kite, or trying to get really good photographs of the birds – his father would, without saying anything, put in an expert oar: the kite, for instance, would then take on all kinds of unexpected dimensions. Train remembered one kite that had lights for night-flying and a bigger one that carried a little camera and took aerial shots.

The island was very near now. Train could see the girl clearly, looking towards them. Even at this distance he could see that she was shy, withdrawn, private-looking. But pretty.

The boat struck shingle and people were shouting to each other and the holiday was really starting.

*

By that evening, Train and Mee were friends. Pog brought them together. Train's father said, 'Train! Here a minute!' and Pog looked puzzled, then began to make steam-engine noises. He tugged at Mee's hand and said, 'Not a train. A big boy.'

So Train explained that his name was Frederick Traynor. Mee explained that her name was Amelia and Pog's name was Timothy.

Train's father introduced himself to Mee's mother by blurting out, 'Do you like curry?'

'Curry? Oh, yes . . . I think so.'

'Well, you won't like ours,' he replied, happily gloomy. 'It takes the enamel off your teeth. But I could make a mild one, I suppose. Dinner tomorrow, then?'

Mee's mother said yes, but would it be all right if she brought something not curried for Pog? The idea of Pog eating curry somehow became a great joke. Mee saw her mother smile, really smile. For the first time in many months, Train saw his father look a little like he used to look, when Mum was alive.

The sun went down and night came fast. Half a dozen people were talking and drinking round a big camp fire. In the windows of the few half-ruined cottages, lights flickered. Tents were erected, hurricane lamps glowed yellow. The bald man was still perfecting his tent, working slowly and thoroughly, knocking little metal pegs into the ground then taking them out and knocking them in again an inch to the left or right. Pog was asleep. His mother was talking to the pretty foreign girl in the red shirt and Train's father was doing something to a window in the cottage that Mee, her mother and Pog were to occupy for the next two weeks. The two boys and one girl Train had seen on the boat were making a lot of noise, but they were quite a distance away.

Mee and Train squatted on the dewy grass, tending the little fire they had built. Stars glittered in a darker and darker sky. Fires died down, lights in cottages and tents began to go out one by one.

'Mee! Time for bed!'

'Coming!' To Train, she said, 'Well. I'd better go...'

'Tomorrow, then?'

'Oh yes! Tomorrow!'

*

Tomorrow dawned clear, salty, sparkling and fresh as a daisy. The sun lit hard glitters in the sea and made the bald man's head flash glassily. He was the only person, other than Mee and Train, up and about. They saw him a hundred feet below them, squatting on a rock. He was tapping it with a geologist's hammer. His calf muscles bulged whitely in the sun, but the bald dome of his head was whiter still.

'Bet you it burns,' said Train. 'Bright pink by the end of the day.'

'Bet you it doesn't!' said Mee. 'Five pence.'

'Lobster red!' said Train. 'It's bound to! –'

'Five pence,' Mee repeated smugly.

'All right, five pence! But you're throwing money away!'

At that very moment, the bald man picked up the hat that Train had failed to see and put it carefully on his head. It was an amazing hat – a huge, white, wide, peaked muffin divided into segments and with a button at the centre of the crown. He adjusted it until it was straight and level on his head, then picked up his hammer and tapped the rocks again. Tink, tink, tink. Not satisfied, he put the hammer down again and made a further eighth-of-an-inch adjustment to the hat; nodded his head; and got back to work.

'Five p, *if* you please!' said Mee through her laughter.

'Worth double!' choked Train. 'Never seen anything like it! What a man! What a hat!'

'Flat 'At!' Mee giggled.

'Flat 'At! That's what we'll call him!'

Train's father blundered out of the tent, sleepy and crumpled. 'You two were laughing,' he complained. 'It's too early for laughter. Just smile, silently. Good morning, Mee. Any hot water?'

Train pointed to the Primus with the kettle on it and his father said, 'Oh, yes. Good. Shave. What were you laughing at?' 'Come and see.' They led him to where he could look down on the bald man in the amazing hat. Mee began to giggle again. 'Flat 'At,' she explained.

'Flat 'At,' Train's father repeated and Train saw the creases round his mouth deepen with amusement. 'You know who that is?' he said. 'It's none other than Czeslaw, king of the seismologists. Earthquakes, and all that,' he added, for Mee's benefit. 'We call him Chatty Czeslaw,' he went on, 'because he never says a thing. Like me. Not a syllable. He just wallops rocks.'

'Is he any good? At his job, I mean?' Train asked.

'I don't know,' said his father. 'Nobody knows. He never tells us. He's silent and sinister. Well, seismology ought to be sinister . . . All to do with earth tremors, and underground mysteries, and the effects of explosions . . .'

'Perhaps he's a spy?' Mee said. 'Perhaps he's planning to split the world in two and keep the big bit for himself?'

'Almost certainly,' said Train's father. 'A fiend from the other side of the Iron Curtain. Sinister brain, heart of stone. That's what I've always thought him. But now – '

'Now you've seen him in his Flat 'At?' Mee suggested.

'The Flat 'At does change things,' said Mr Traynor.

The kettle boiled over and the Primus spluttered. They ran to it. Train's father poured himself a tin cup of hot water for shaving. Train said, 'Coffee. Shall we make just one big pot?' Mee said, 'Yes. Then we can all share it. Unless your father would rather – '

'Generally, the old man makes for the peaks and sets up his tent in the loneliest place he can find,' Train said. 'This time – ' he pointed to the tent. It was quite close to the cottage. 'One big pot,' he said.

Later in the morning, Flat 'At Czeslaw actually spoke. He went up to Train's father and said, in his high-pitched, hoarse voice, 'Ah! Mister Trrhaynor! See how interrhesting is what I have to show you!' Mee and Train nudged each other, relishing the throaty rollęd Rs and keeping their eyes off the hat, which they knew would make them giggle rudely.

'That *is* interesting,' said Mr Traynor, examining the pieces of rock in Czeslaw's wide, stubby-fingered hand. The fragments were black, flecked with gold. The two men began to talk the jargon of their profession. Train and Mee lost interest and chased Pog about. He squeaked and yelped happily, crying 'No! No!' when they caught him and tickled him. When they stopped tickling him he cried 'Do again!' and ran away.

When Czeslaw and his hat had gone, Train asked

his father, 'Are the stones he found really interesting?'

Mr Traynor said, 'Well, yes. By which I mean no. Pretty, anyway. Nice little gold flecks – cuprous – in a black basalt. You wouldn't find them everywhere. But you're bound to find them here.'

'Why?'

'Because the island is more or less *made* of the stuff!'

'Then why did Czeslaw find the stones interesting?'

'Well, he's a seismologist, not a petrologist like me, so I suppose – hell, I don't know. And belonging to the S.I.I. gives him the chance to look around the place. He tells me that the deposits and stones in this region have always been of ''ghrreat interhrrest'' to him and his friends –'

'I think they're interesting,' said Mee's mother, joining them, 'The stones, I mean. Let me look. Very interesting. Jewellery!'

'Jewellery?' said Mee.

'You could make a terrific bracelet and necklace from the rounded ones,' said her mother. 'The ones polished and rounded by the sea!'

'You're right!' said Mee, staring at the stones. 'Train! Let's try and find some! A whole set of them all matched!'

Pog said, 'Me too.'

And that is how, two days later, Train, Mee and Pog came to be squatting on a stony shore overhung by a great black rock, filling a Smarties tube with matched black and gold stones: and how the three of them made the discovery that could change the whole world.

*

'Help me!' Mee said. 'Hang on to it! It's lifting like mad!'

He put his hands over hers. She cried, 'No! One hand on the cap! It will fly off if you don't!'

Train did as she told him. He felt the tube thrust upwards against his strength, as if it were a rocket trying to take off.

'This is impossible!' he said. 'It can't possibly be – '

'Just hang on!' said Mee. 'Hang on, that's all!'

They hung on. 'My arms are getting tired,' Mee said. Train grunted. 'Mine too. But it doesn't change . . . I mean, the force doesn't change, the tube doesn't push harder or softer, it just keeps pushing.'

'My red stone,' said Pog, interested.

'Shut up, Pog!' said Train. 'Look, we can't hold it like this for ever . . . we've got to *do* something!'

'We could just let go.'

'Not on your life. This is something important. I'm not letting it go.'

'What, then?'

'I've got it! All we need do is, keep a firm grip on the tube . . . and raise it until it touches the rock hanging over us! Then we can let go! The tube will just stick itself against the rock!'

'All right. Ready?'

'Ready. Carefully, now.'

They slowly allowed the tube to pull their arms straight up above their heads and edged sideways until they stood on a hump of rock. The hump made them tall enough to touch the ceiling of rock above them. The cap of the tube touched this ceiling.

'Shall we let go now?' said Mee.

'Yes, but slowly. We'll take our hands away slowly, right?'

They unlaced their fingers one by one. At last their hands were free. They dropped their arms.

'Phew!'

'Phew!'

The tube stuck, immobile, to the rock ceiling. They stared at it, silently, until Pog said, 'My red stone. Mine!'

'Yes, I know, Pog,' said Train. 'But hush for a moment. I'm thinking.'

'*My* red stone,' Pog insisted.

Mee bit her lip and stared at the tube. 'What does it all mean, Train?'

'Pinch me,' he replied.

She pinched him. He said, 'Ouch. All right, we're not dreaming. But it's mad all the same. We've discovered Antigrav.'

'In the tube,' Pog said. 'Mine. Oh yes, mine!' He began to cry.

'Antigrav . . . ?' said Mee.

'Antigrav means Antigravity – something that cuts off the pull of gravity. I mean, we're all held to the Earth by gravity, the pull from the centre of the Earth. That's why we stay on the ground. If there was no gravity we'd just drift off into space or float about like spacemen.'

'I know all that,' said Mee. 'But it's not just Antigrav we've got. That tubeful of stones was *pulling* away from Earth. It was lifting, lifting like mad.'

Pog said, 'My *stone*!' They took no notice. He rubbed his fists in his eyes and walked away.

'I suppose you're right,' Train said to Mee. 'Antigrav wouldn't *pull* like that, would it? And anyhow, Antigrav is impossible. It's just an old story-book idea – just another impossible dream, like perpetual motion.'

They stared at the tube, silent again. They did not see Pog come back carrying a long stick blanched by sea and sun. 'My stone!' he said – and swung the stick at the Smarties tube.

'Don't!' shouted Mee and Train. Too late! By a chance in a hundred, Pog's aim was perfect. The tip of the stick hit the tube and knocked it sideways. There was a light, fast spattering sound as the stones, released, shot out, rat-tat-tatting at the rock ceiling then falling down. A half second later, the empty tube fell from the ceiling and lay on the sand at their feet. Some of the stones made little clicking noises bouncing off rock as they fell. Most just dropped silently into the sand.

Pog walked straight to a dimple in the sand, bent

down, picked something up and said 'Pog's stone.' He opened his hand, and there was the red stone.

'You little moron!' screamed Train. He was so angry that he could have hit Pog. 'The most exciting thing in the world and you have to . . . !'

Mee said, 'It's all right, Train, it's all right, don't you see? We can do it again! Come and help me!'

She began picking up the black and gold stones. Train, still fuming, joined her. 'I've got one,' he said. 'I've got two!' said Pog – and so he had.

'Put them in the Smarties tube,' said Mee. 'Just as they were. Oh, here's another. *And* another. The tube's almost full.'

'Does it have to be completely full?' said Train, thoughtfully.

'I don't see why it has to be. Let's find out. Pog, darling . . . !'

'My stone!' said Pog, backing away.

'Ah, come on, Pog, just for a moment! Lend us your lovely red stone! We'll give it back, that's a promise. Cross my heart!'

Pog imitated her action, dubiously: and at last, held out his red stone. 'Ready with the tube?' Mee asked Train.

'Ready. All filled up with black-and-golds. It's not lifting, or anything. It's just a tube nearly full of stones.'

'All right. Keep well under the ceiling. Ready . . . steady . . . go!'

She dropped the red stone in and Train slapped on the cap and clamped his thumb over it.

She did not have to ask him if the trick worked a

second time: she needed only to see the muscles in his arms stand out, his face redden and his eyes go wide.

*

Half an hour later, they knew much more about their discovery.

'It was eight black and gold stones last time, wasn't it?' said Train. 'Well, this time we'll use only four. I've stuck an aluminium tube in the Smarties tube to strengthen it.'

'Why not just use the aluminium and throw away the Smarties tube?' Mee asked.

Train said, 'I don't know. I think it's because the Smarties tube looks more . . . innocent. Childish. You ready?'

'Ready,' said Mee. 'Pog, this time you can do it. That's right, drop your red stone in. In she goes!'

'And up she goes!' muttered Train as the tube pulled in his hands.

'Is it pulling as much?'

'Nothing like as much. Here, take over and feel for yourself. We were right. The fewer black and gold stones, the less the pull.'

Mee took the tube. She began to turn her wrist as if she were pointing the beam of a torch at various spots. 'It's funny,' she reported, 'doing this makes the pull stronger or weaker. Try it.'

Train said, 'Let's try it outside, away from the cave. Perhaps the pull has something to do with where we stand, or the rocks above us . . .'

They walked about the beach, Train holding the tube and keeping his arm uplifted in the direction of the strongest pull.

'It always comes from the same direction,' he said. 'But there's nothing up there. Not even a cloud.'

Pog, trotting patiently where they led, said 'Man in the Moon'. Mee and Train hardly heard him. They frowned at the tube and at the empty sky, pondering.

'Hallo, Man!' said Pog, pointing to the sky.

This time they heard him. Up in the blue sky, where Pog was pointing, they could just make out the faint, daylight silver-gold ghost of the moon.

*

Mee's mother and Train's father were crouched over a cluster of rocks that made a rough table between her cottage and his tent. He was preparing tonight's curry, pounding small yellow seeds to powder with a stone.

'Alan,' she said, 'are you really going to eat that?'

'Of course. And so, Peg, will you. So will Mee. So will Train. Only Pog is excused. He is too young to die.' A sudden breeze blew a little cloud of yellow powder into his nose. He sneezed violently. Peg laughed.

'Coriander, cardomum, chillies . . .' Alan Traynor said, opening another jar of little coloured seeds. 'Eye of newt and toe of frog,' said Peg.

'I once played one of the witches in Macbeth,' said Alan, continuing his pounding and mixing. 'It was in a school play. My wig was made of unravelled string and I put half a walnut shell in each eye. I was very good indeed,' he said seriously, eyeing Peg as if to challenge her to say that he wasn't.

'I'm sure you were,' she said, sweetly. 'Go easy on those chillies! I can only take so much. Yesterday's curry was like eating volcanoes.'

'Very good indeed,' Alan repeated. 'I remember what the review in the local paper said of my performance: they called it "uninhibited".'

Peg looked at deep creases round Alan's mouth and the permanent frown between his kind eyes. Quietly, she said, 'And when did you become inhibited?'

He pounded vigorously at the seeds, without looking up and answered, 'At about the same time you did, I suppose. And for the same reasons.'

Peg said 'Oh –' and nothing else for half a minute. Then she said, 'Were you happy with your wife?'

'Very. Were you happy with your husband?'

'Yes.'

'Well, there you are then.' He looked at her and said, 'The recipe calls for *some* chillies, Peg.'

'Oh, all right then,' she laughed. 'Do your worst.'

He picked up the little dish containing the ground chillies and threw it over his shoulder.

'Why did you do that?' Peg said, shocked.

'Good for the ants. Liven them up.'

'No, why?'

'If I were a younger man,' Alan said, 'I'd invite you out to pubs and discotheques and the movies or whatever. There's nothing of that sort on the island, and I'm not a younger man. I am an older man. The most I can think of to offer is – no chillies.'

Peg said, 'I see.' She thought for a while and added, 'Well, I'm not exactly a "younger woman".'

'Then you shouldn't go around looking like one,' said Alan, busily pounding.

He looked up anxiously at her and said, 'That was supposed to be a compliment.'

'I know. It was very nice. You needn't scowl like that.'

'I always scowl when I'm embarrassed.'

'You mean, I embarrass you? That's rather a strange thing to say!'

'I think you know perfectly well what I'd *like* to say, but that would embarrass me even more.'

She thought this over, and eventually said, 'Yes. Well . . . I suppose I should reply, "Why, Alan! I hardly know you!" – but that wouldn't do because I think I do know you. And besides – '

He said, 'Besides, there's the children to consider. We're not alone.'

She nodded. Then she said, 'We *are* alone! Where have the children got to? Shouldn't we go and find them?'

'I'll find them when I've finished this. You'll come too?'

'Of course!' With her toe, she stirred a grain of powder on the ground, and smiled.

*

'Three more stones, Pog!' Train said. 'Little ones, mind. That's right, put them in the bucket. Now let's try it!'

They had used the drawstring from Pog's bathing trunks to tie the Smarties tube to Pog's bucket. The bucket had stones in it. The Smarties tube stood straight up in the air, pulling at the cord. Mee kept the bucket from rising into the air.

Pog put the second of three stones in . . . Mee said, 'Whoa! Stop! I think that's it! Let's try!' She took her fingers from the edge of the bucket – nervously at first, ready to hold on again if anything went wrong. Nothing did. The bucket swayed very gently, six inches from the ground.

Train said 'Wow!' He picked up the bucket and held it shoulder high. As he lifted it, the Smarties pack rose, keeping the cord taut. He let go of the bucket and stood back. Exactly balanced by its own weight and the upward pull of the stones in the Smarties pack, the bucket hovered. The children stared.

A puff of wind pushed the bucket. It swayed on its cord, rocked gently and began to move out towards the sea. They walked after it – 'No! Don't touch it! Let's see what happens!' Still rocking gently, it moved on seawards.

Mee got between it and the water. 'Tennis, anyone?' she said, and very gently pushed the bucket inland. It glided slowly and perfectly to Train. With his fingertips, he pushed it back to Mee. 'Tennis, oh yes!' said Pog.

Another puff of wind, stronger this time. The bucket swayed, rocked like a pendulum – and began, very slowly, to sink. They watched it.

'Why did it do that?' said Mee.

'Don't know,' said Train, watching the seesawing bucket come nearer and nearer the ground. 'Oh yes, I do, though!' He steadied the bucket and the Smarties tube. It no longer rocked. It stayed exactly a foot from the ground.

'Why?' said Mee.

'It must be the moon, don't you see? When the bucket and the tube started rocking about, each swing made the Smarties tube *not* point straight at the moon. So the pull of the moon altered all the time, with each swing, and the bucket sank. Now I've stopped the swinging, there's a constant pull and it's all right again.'

'My stone did it,' said Pog. 'Red.'

'You're right, Pog, it's your red stone!' Train said. 'Magic!'

'Oh yes,' said Pog. 'Maggidge.'

*

Two hundred or three hundred yards away, white-legged, black-socked Arthur Sonning and red-shirted Myra Pryzsyck were walking, picking their way over the black boulders that burst through the thick, mossy grass of the island. 'Beautiful!' he grumbled. 'You really are beautiful!'

'You are very kind,' said Myra for perhaps the tenth time. She was hot, bored and nearly angry. She wished she had not worn her red shirt, a light colour would not absorb so much heat. She wished she had not done her hair in a topknot, it made her head to – what was the word? – scratch? – no, *itch*. Scratch was the word for what had happened to her leg; the smooth brown was spoiled by an untidy red claw-mark made by a gorse bush. She wished Arthur Sonning had not asked her, yet again, to come for a walk. She wished he would not wear black socks. She wished they could stop walking, but if they stopped walking, he'd talk still more.

'I realize I'm not much to look at, but you're beautiful!' Arthur said, making it sound like a complaint. 'The very first time we met – that November evening, the International Science Congress, do you remember? – I said, ''She's beautiful!'' And then we met again, the first day on this island. And I helped you with your rucksack –'

'You were very kind,' said Myra, wearily. His voice went on and on.

It was when he took her arm – held it in his fingers – that Myra felt inside her the slight, pleasurable 'snap' of her temper breaking. A small red flush appeared on her high cheekbones; she began to pull out, one by one, the hairpins that held her topknot in place and poked them viciously between her teeth for safe keeping. She let her hair and tongue free.

'Mr Sonning,' she said, 'You talk so very much' (hairpin) 'and you mean so very little' (hairpin). 'Especially to me, Mr Sonning' (hairpin). 'To me, you mean *nothing*, but *nothing at all*!' (hairpin). 'You keep saying "Do you remember this?" and "Do you remember that?" and "Will you come for a walk" so that you can tell me how very beautful I am and how very ugly you are – and, Mr Sonning,' (the last two hairpins) 'I quite agree! I am a pretty girl, Mr Sonning, and you are not a pretty man, and I am finding you very boring! And what do you have to say to that, Mr Sonning?'

Arthur Sonning went a strange colour and kept walking. His voice no longer whined when next he spoke. He said, 'I'd like to ask you just one thing, Myra. I will be going for a walk tomorrow. Will you come?'

'No!' shouted Myra. 'I bloody will not, do you hear me? No more the bloody walking!'

Arthur Sonning walked a little faster. Still not looking at Myra, he said, imitating her accent, 'I think you bloody will, Myra.'

'And what makes you think so?'

'You're a great walker, Myra. You've got to be. I mean, it wasn't very long ago that you went for a really long walk, didn't you? Half across Europe. You said good-bye to your friends, good-bye to the Party, good-bye even to your family – '

Myra flinched but said nothing.

'Of course I've got it a bit wrong, haven't I? You

never said "good-bye", you just went. Made a bolt for it. Oh, I don't blame you, things are very difficult for you. And sometimes you think of making a bolt for it again – in the opposite direction. You're all mixed up, aren't you? Because nobody trusts you, on either side. You need someone to make your mind up for you, Myra.'

Myra said, 'I have met people like you so often, you nasty little man! I can deal with you!' But her voice shook.

Arthur said, 'Can you deal with *him*, Myra?'

At first, she did not understand what he meant. But then, following his finger, she picked out a distant figure squatting on the rocks; a powerful figure, wearing an absurd flat hat.

'That's right,' Arthur said. 'Friend Czeslaw. I mean, he could be your friend, Myra. He wants to be your friend. You've done scientific work that only people like Czeslaw can understand and appreciate. In the old days, over there.'

'The work I did,' Myra said. 'I came to know was wrong. Very wrong. That is why I left –'

'So now you're a sort of laboratory assistant, getting nowhere fast. And with all that good work locked up inside you, Myra! And Czeslaw wanting you back! And he's not your only friend, Myra. There's Old Smoothie, for instance.'

'Old Smoothie?'

'Leo Alexander,' Arthur said, looking sideways at Myra. 'Doctor Leo Alexander, the well-known TV personality and fellow-traveller! Don't tell me you didn't know!'

'I did not know!'

'Of course not, if you say so . . . There's a lot of us, Myra. Join us again, and you'd be on the right side. The winning side. Take my advice –'

'I can do without you, Mr Sonning.'

'Yeah. But I'm not sure Czeslaw and the others on our side are willing to do without you, Myra. I mean, if you started opening your mouth about the work you did in the old days – or if we started telling your new friends a few things about your past – Why, Myra! You're trembling!'

She said, 'And what do you get out of all this, Mr Sonning?'

'Why, I get what I want most, Myra! You! I love you!'

She stared at him, then began to run.

He called after her, 'OK for a walk tomorrow, then?'

She ran on, blindly.

*

'Come for a walk!' suggested Dr Leo Alexander, flashing his nice teeth and crinkling his black-lashed grey eyes. In close-up, on colour TV, his eyes were quite hypnotic.

'Oh, *I can't* Leo! I'm sort of committed to this curry!' said Peg. She laughed feebly and pointed at a mess of dishes, pots and stoves all around her on the rocks and grass.

'Never mind all that!' said Leo, boyishly. 'Come for a walk! I want you to!'

'Oh . . .' said Peg, thinking how much she owed Leo.

'And there's something I want to talk to you about,' Leo smiled. 'Something quite important.'

'Is it to do with Pog and Mee?'

'Nothing that important!' Leo said, laughing easily. 'But important all the same. Important to *me*, Peg.'

'I suppose I ought to know what Pog and Mee are up to . . .' she said uncertainly: and went with him.

*

Mee and Train were still experimenting with the bucket and Smarties tube. Pog was being a train. He went 'CHH-ch-ch-ch, CHH-ch-ch-ch,' and occasionally hooted 'Wooo-ooo!' for the whistle.

'What I don't understand', said Mee, 'is that he's never seen a steam train. No more have you. Or I. Well, except on TV. Yet Pog still thinks of trains in steam-engine noises. All the kids of his age do – they talk about ''Choo-choos''. I wonder why?'

'Look at this, Mee,' Train said. He had taken several stones out of the bucket. It was now loaded too lightly for the pull of the Smarties tube: if Train had let go of the bucket, it would have risen straight up, fast. But he had rigged the tube so that it was hanging at an angle. Bits of stick and rag kept it from pulling itself upright, in line with the moon.

He let go of the bucket and it began to turn and spin without rising. 'See?' said Train, 'the tube is trying to get itself straight, and point at the moon. But it can't, so it spins.'

'Fantastic,' Mee said, vaguely. She was watching Pog, not the bucket. Pog was trying to be a locomotive reversing, but kept tripping on stones and falling over backwards.

'No, *listen*, Mee!' said Train. 'Never mind Pog and puffer trains, I've got a real engine here! Look at it! Think!'

She did as she was told . . . The bucket spun . . . Train poked at it with his fingertip now and again to make sure that it neither rose nor fell. The bucket spun faster and faster. It whirled.

'Don't you see?' said Train . . . 'It's an *engine*! It's spinning, it's developing power!'

'It's certainly going round and round,' said Mee.

'But you don't *see*! We've discovered *free power*! If you made a proper machine, with Pog's pebble and all the rest of it in the middle, you could drive other machines! For nothing! It's a revolution!'

Pog fell down backwards on a sharp stone and howled. Mee ran to him. Train sighed, and muttered, 'I'll make a model boat and strap the tube in at an angle. If I'm right, the boat will go along all by itself.'

Mee said 'Poor Pog! Where's the pain?' and Pog, enjoying the attention, howled louder than ever and pointed importantly at his bottom.

*

'What was that?' said Peg, clutching Leo's arm.

'What was what?'

'That yell. It sounded like Pog! It was Pog!'

'Look, Peg, try and forget Pog and the rest of them for just one tiny minute. I was telling you about something very important.'

'I don't think I like what you were telling me, Leo. I'm not political, and I don't think science should be political, and I don't want to be involved with it – or you, I suppose, which sounds ungrateful . . . That *is* Pog!'

She ran to the edge of a cliff so that she could look over the shore, where the noise came from. She could see Pog easily, and Mee squatting by him, attending to him.

'Mee! What's happening?' Peg shouted.

Mee shouted something Peg couldn't hear. Train was some distance from Mee and Pog, Peg saw, and her heart stopped thumping. If it had been anything serious, Train would have left what he was doing.

'*What's – wrong – with – Pog?*' shouted Peg.

'Nothing!' shouted Mee, her voice almost lost against the breeze. 'He's all right!'

Leo said, 'What's up? Is he all right?'

'Oh yes, I think – I don't know.'

'Ah!' said Leo, 'I'll solve the mystery!' He fumbled in the inside pocket of his light jacket and pulled out a pair of miniature binoculars, hardly bigger than a pack of cigarettes. 'Got them for nothing,' he said, putting them to his eyes and focusing. 'Mentioned them on a "Science Now" programme, and the makers gave them to me.'

He fiddled with the focusing wheel. 'There you are!' he said, handing them to Peg. 'See for yourself!'

She looked through them. A large Pog jumped into vision, red-faced and earnest. As she watched, Mee twisted him towards her, pulling up his bathing trunks to exhibit his wound. The binoculars were so good that Peg could see a reddish bump and a deeper red scratch. She saw Mee's face, laughing, and Mee's finger pointing at the damaged area. Then Mee picked up a sharp stone and held it up and pointed again at Pog's bottom.

'He fell on a stone and scratched himself,' Peg told Leo, 'and he's making a big thing of it, the baby! Well, he is a baby . . . What incredible binoculars! Here, your turn.' She handed them back to Leo, and waved to Mee.

'Incredible,' said Leo. 'But not made by *us*: made by *them*. Which is what I was talking about, Peg. What I was trying to make you understand. The future isn't in *our* hands, it's with the nations who really get to grips with science and . . .'

His voice tailed off. Through the binoculars, he had picked up Train. The binoculars were so powerful that the image jiggled. Leo had to sit down and lock his elbows and thighs into a firm triangle before he could convince himself that he really was seeing what he thought he saw . . .

Train, frowning with concentration.

A toy bucket with stones in it.

A lash-up of bits of driftwood, rags and a white drawstring.

A brightly coloured cylinder, a cardboard tube that had held sweets.

All this spinning slowly, a foot above the ground, with nothing holding it up or keeping it down; spinning slowly, then faster, then faster still.

'What are you looking at, Leo?'

'Just trying out the binoculars. I won't be a moment. Walk on, if you like.'

'I'll see if I can find a way down the cliff, and make sure that Pog really is all right,' said Peg.

'Yes, you do that.'

She left. Leo, hardly breathing, kept his binoculars rock-steady and stared through them.

*

'Look at old Smoothie Leo. Even on this little island, he's still the TV personality.'

Mee looked where Train pointed. In the golden, slanting light of the evening Leo was standing over Peg who was busy again with the curry.

'He's changed for dinner,' Mee giggled. 'Next thing you know, he'll wear his medals and one of those cocked hats with feathers in it!'

'Makes my Pop look shabby,' said Train. He was right. Beside Leo, in his white jacket, beautifully creased cream trousers and expertly tied silk neck-scarf, Alan Traynor looked a tramp. His shirt hung out at the back, because he had been bending over cooking pots. The soles of his bare feet were stained bright green from the grass. His lean arms, blackish brown from the sun, pumped vigorously at a Primus stove. As he pumped, he stared upwards, frowning, at Leo.

'My argument is', said Leo, waving a glass containing a golden drink, 'that Science is Power and Power is Science. I can't see how anyone with even a notion of history can disagree with a basic argument like that!'

'I'm not arguing,' said Mr Traynor. 'I'm merely thinking it would be nice if you offered me a drink.'

'My dear fellow! – ' said Leo, producing a leather and silver hip flask. 'Have you got a glass?' Without speaking, Alan tossed him an enamel mug. Leo raised an eyebrow, shrugged, and poured.

'Science,' said Alan Traynor, 'isn't just power. Science is *science*. I do my work not to gain power, or give power to someone or something, but simply to find things out.'

'But surely you must consider how the things you find out are used?' said Leo.

'Not my job,' said Mr Traynor. 'Science is my job.'

'But if you discovered – oh, I don't know, a new source of power, or something absolutely vital like that – wouldn't you have to consider who used it, and for what? Here, Czeslaw! Help me! Tell Traynor the facts of life about science and power!'

Czeslaw stopped – he was on his solitary way to his tent – and said 'Mr T-hrraynor!' (a little bow).

'Miss Amelia!' (a bow to Mee, who smiled uneasily). 'Colleagues!' (a bow to the men). 'What were you saying, Doctor Alexander?'

'I was trying to convince poor old Traynor here that science is power, and power is science. I mean, the whole of history shows – '

'So,' said Czeslaw.

'Yes. I'm sure you understand what I mean. I was arguing that – '

Peg forced a smile and cut in. 'Don't bother with these idiots, Mr Czeslaw, they're arguing like rather silly sixth-formers!'

'I am not bothered,' said Czeslaw, massively.

'But you must have an *opinion*,' objected Leo.

'I have an opinion,' said Czeslaw. 'My opinion is that it is better to *do* about these things, than to *talk*.'

He held up his hammer and waggled it under Leo's nose, almost as if it were a weapon; bowed to Peg; and walked away.

Leo looked startled, then ran after Czeslaw. Mee and Train heard what Leo said: 'But, Czeslaw, I don't think you quite understand what – ' He glanced sideways at the children, and said 'I must talk to you, Czeslaw!'

Czeslaw grunted and walked on, leaving Leo to follow him.

*

In the middle of the curry dinner Pog appeared. Peg tried to shoo him back to bed, but he stood firm on his dignity and would not be moved. Blinking in the light of the hurricane and calor-gas lamps, he said, 'No bed. Time to get up.'

'But it's not time to get up, Pog, it's late! It's night!'

'*You're* all up!' Pog accused. 'So *I'm* all up. And I hurt.'

'Oh no you don't! You're fibbing!' his mother said.

'Hurt!' Pog repeated.

'Where? Show me!'

Pog thought for a moment and then, inspired, pulled down his pyjama trousers and showed the almost invisible wound on his bottom. 'Train did it,' he said.

'Me!' Train yelped. 'What do you mean, me! I never touched you!'

Mee laughed. 'He means choo-choo train, don't you Pog? When you were being a train and fell down?'

'Oh, yes!' said Pog. His mouth went down and his brow puckered as he tried to find words to explain things to his mother.

'I was a train, and Train was just . . . just Train . . .' Realizing that this made no sense, he added, 'Train with the bucket. Maggidge. It flew by itself. Train and Mee did it. But was my stone. Pog's stone, the red one!'

Peg shrugged, laughed, kissed Pog and sat him on her lap. The others smiled. But Train burst out and said, 'He should go to bed! He ought to be asleep!'

Everyone stared at Train, shocked. His father said, 'Hey, steady on!' and, to take attention away from his son's outburst said, 'Go on, Pog! Tell us about the "maggidge"!'

'He means "magic",' said Mee.

'Yes, I guessed that. What's all this about buckets and "maggidge", Pog?'

'There was Train, and Mee, and Pog,' said Pog, his face twisted with the effort of making everything clear, 'and the bucket. And the Smartie stones. And my red maggidge stone. And it – and it – and it went up in the air and stayed there!'

While he talked, Train nudged Mee. She said 'Oh!' and jumped to her feet. 'I'll take him to bed!' she said to her mother. 'Come on, Pog! Time for bed!' She scooped him up and almost ran with him to the cottage.

'Well . . . !' said her mother. 'How very anxious everyone is about Pog's bedtime!' There was a howl from the cottage. 'Oh, Lord!' said Peg. 'I suppose I'll have to get him settled down.'

So Train and his father were left alone. 'What *is* all this, Train? All this hushing-up? What's Pog trying to say? Did you do something to him?'

'No! of course not!'

'*Something* happened. Something about buckets, and magic, and Pog's red stone. What's the guilty secret?'

'It's *not* a guilty secret. I've told you that.'

'But you don't want to tell?'

'No.'

Alan Traynor sighed. Peg and Mee came back.

The curry dinner went on, but it wasn't very good fun after all.

*

Next day, Mee and Train lay in the cave, out of the sun. Pog played on the shore. Mee said, 'Why didn't you want to tell your father?'

'I don't really know. I've been thinking a lot about the Antigrav thing . . . The more I think about it, the bigger it gets in my mind. I don't want to tell anyone, not even my old man.'

'But he's the one person you *could* tell! I mean, he's – he's – '

'I know what you mean, but I don't want to tell even him.'

'But why not?'

'Because it's such a huge thing! It could mean anything! – anything at all! I mean, I was raving on yesterday about it being a source of power – you know, unlimited free power to drive machines and all that – but it could mean even more than that.'

'*What* could it mean?'

'I don't know, I don't know!'

'Your father would know, he'd sort it all out for you – '

'But he's not the only person on this island.'

She stared at him. 'What do you mean by *that*!' she said.

'Well, there's Flat 'At Czeslaw – no, don't laugh, I know his hat is funny, but I don't think he is. Nor does my old man. Before we came here, he was muttering something about this holiday being like a party for the Party – you know, the Party people on the other side.'

'He was just making a joke. He makes jokes like that.'

'Czeslaw isn't a joke. I know he's not and you know he's not.'

Mee thought, and said, 'Well, that's only one person. Who are the others?'

'That girl Myra and her boy friend.'

'What, just because she's foreign? And pretty? The deadly woman spy who traps all the men? You must be joking!'

'My father mentioned her when he talked about Czeslaw. Czeslaw's her boss. Did you know that?'

'Well, anyhow, that creepy Sonning person isn't Myra's boy friend. She goes for walks with him and all that, but she hates him.'

'If he's a creep, why does she go for walks with him?'

'I don't know,' Mee admitted.

'And how do you know she hates him?' Train insisted.

'I don't know that, either,' Mee said, 'except that I *do* know. She sort of cringes from him. I can't explain it . . .'

'And I can't explain why I feel I shouldn't tell anyone at all – not even Dad – about our discovery,' said Train.

They were silent for a minute, then Mee said, 'Well, that only makes three.'

'Three what?'

'Three people to be worried about . . . Three of *Them*. Czeslaw, Arthur Sonning and Myra.'

'There's another.'

'Who?'

'Leo.'

She looked at him wide-eyed, and then began to laugh. 'Leo!' she hooted. 'Doctor Leo Alexander! You really think he's one of *Them*, one of the baddies? Honestly, Train!'

'There you are, you see!' said Train, furious. 'You don't think! You just laugh like an idiot and refuse to think!'

'But *Leo* . . . !' said Mee, still laughing.

'Yes, Leo!' shouted Train. 'Leo, the TV personality! Suppose he found out about our Antigrav! Don't you think he'd want it for himself? Can't you see him doing the big star turn on telly, with a chromium-plated Smarties tube and Pog's red pebble?'

'Oh,' said Mee, and stopped laughing.

'And what did he mean last night, when he was talking about Science being Power, and Power being Science?'

'He's always going on about that,' Mee interrupted. 'It's nothing new. One of his Big Questions that Demand an Answer.'

'All right, but why did he say, ''suppose someone discovered the secret of infinite power'', or whatever the words were? And why did he chase after Czeslaw and want to have a talk with him? Why Czeslaw? Czeslaw never talks to anyone, and Czeslaw had just shut Leo up –'

'There could be a million reasons why,' said Mee, uncertainly.

'Or there could be only one,' said Train. 'Leo could have spotted us mucking about with the bucket and everything. *Anyone* could have spotted us! It's a tiny little island, and there we were playing with our new toy right out in the open – '

Mee said, in a very small voice, 'Leo's got binoculars.'

'What do you mean?'

'He got Mother to go for a walk with him yesterday – Leo's been very good to us, she can't very well refuse – and I asked her if she enjoyed the walk, and she didn't answer properly, she just changed the subject by talking about Leo's super-de-luxe miniature binoculars. He was using them when we were on the shore,' said Mee, miserably. 'When Pog hurt himself. When my mother and Leo were above us, on the cliff. I saw him using his binoculars. Looking at us.'

'And I was playing with the Antigrav,' said Train, in a whisper. 'I'd just got it working perfectly – you know, spinning round and round. I remember it perfectly. And that very moment, Leo was watching . . . I wonder how much he saw?'

'Everything,' said Mee. 'Because he went on watching while Mother was clambering about on the cliff, trying to get down to us. She told me. He said, ''You go on, I'm busy with my binoculars.'' He watched you for a long time.'

They were silent again. Outside the cave in the

sun, hotter than ever, Pog was being a jet plane. The sea sparkled.

At last, Mee said, 'I think you'd better tell your father after all.'

Train said, 'Yes. I think I'd jolly well better. Right now.'

*

Train looked for and found his father, who was talking to Peg. Train opened his mouth to speak, but didn't: there seemed to be a wall marked PRIVATE round the man and woman. They had not noticed him, so Train stood there trying not to listen.

'I'm talking about us,' said his father. 'Us, not Leo. To hell with Leo.'

'But *I've* got to think about him and talk about him,' Peg said. 'It's only fair. Besides, everyone's against him – '

'Only his intimate friends,' said Alan. 'Everyone else loves him.'

'Oh, shut *up*! It's just that people don't understand him. There are two sides to him. There's Leo the Lion – you know, the TV Leo, all charm and ''Let's Make Science Simple!'' – and there's the other Leo, the Leo who helped me when I most needed it, and stuck by me when everyone else seemed too busy. Got me a job, made it possible for me and the children to keep going. Without Leo – '

'I'm not here to talk about Leo,' Alan repeated.

'Well, that's too bad. And I wish you wouldn't knock him all the time. I owe him a lot.'

'I know you do. All I'm afraid of is that you might actually want to repay him. By giving him yourself. By marrying him instead of me!'

'Well . . . it's sort of half understood that Leo and I might marry – '

'Sort of half understood, is it?' said Alan, bitterly. Under his breath, he swore luridly.

'I heard that!' Peg said. 'Language of that sort! . . .'

'Oh, look, for heaven's sake, this is serious, I'm deadly serious, you can't just – '

'Of course, Leo can't make wonderful curries like you, and he's not a *real* scientist like you – though he seems to do all right for himself with his own particular brand of science – '

'Blasted TV witch-doctor' muttered Alan. He began furiously to pump a Primus and throw pots about. He made so much noise that Train could get away unnoticed.

Antigrav would have to wait for another time.

*

Train wandered about the island, head down and eyes seeing nothing. When Mee appeared beside him, he started. She said, 'What's up?'

'Nothing. I was just thinking.'

'Thinking about what?'

'Nothing.'

She walked beside him silently and then said,

'You were thinking about my mother and your father.'

He stopped and blurted out, 'How did you know that?'

'Oh, just a guess. You saw them talking an hour or so ago – so did I – and you were thinking about them and whether they are going to get married.'

'But – how did you know about this marriage lark?' he gasped.

'It's obvious. Ever since we came here, they've been sort of radiating whatever-it-is. I don't know how you managed *not* to know! And Leo has been hanging around on the fringe smiling a lot and looking handsome. Do you really mean to tell me that you hadn't guessed what was happening? They'll end up married, your papa and my mama!'

'Cor,' said Train. 'What it is to be female!'

'Well?' said Mee, calmly. 'What about it? What do you think?'

'*Married*? I don't know . . .'

'You'd have Pog for a baby brother and me for a sister,' said Mee, doing a cartwheel on the grass. 'Lucky old you!' she said, and did another, so that her face was hidden.

Train just stared at her and said, 'You seem quite cheerful about it!'

'So would you be if you were me, living under the threat of having to call Leo ''Daddy''!' said Mee.

'Leo again . . .' Train said, gloomily.

'You said he's a crook,' said Mee, doing a final cartwheel. 'A villain. You said so. And Antigrav is something worth being crooked about. There's Antigrav, and Czeslaw, and Leo, and us. Myra and Arthur as well, probably. All on this island. Well?'

'Well, what? I'm lost. What are we supposed to do?'

'I don't know,' said Mee. 'Wait for something to happen, I suppose.'

'A minute ago you were turning cartwheels.'

'Why not? I'll do another if you like!' She did another, then put her hands on her hips and stared out at the sea. She sighed, and said, 'I don't know. Do you?'

'No.'

At that moment, a distant voice called 'Cooee!' They turned to face the call. A red shirt gleamed and a brown arm waved. It was Myra, smiling.

*

'Very few people!' said Myra. 'We are being selfish, you know? We do not want all the others. Not all of them.' She waved a hand at the cottage in the distance where the other children were hooting and screeching. Train made a face.

'Of course, if you would like them to come . . .' said Myra.

'No thanks,' said Mee, hastily. Train said, 'We've not even spoken to them really. And as it's a small boat – '

'Oh, very small!' smiled Myra. 'But big enough for our party. That is, for you two – and me – your father, Train – and Doctors Alexander and Czeslaw.'

'A pity Pog can't come,' said Mee.

'Ah, but he is so young and your mother thinks it better he should stay with her. If the sea is to be rough, you know?'

'There's a pretty lift to her voice when she says "You know?" at the end of a sentence,' thought Train. As Myra talked, he stared across at the other island, Luish. He felt a stir of excitement at the thought of setting foot on it. He also felt a pull of caution. There could be a reason behind Myra's trip to Luish. But *what* reason? His father was coming. But then, so was Czeslaw. He said, 'Is Arthur Sonning coming, Myra?'

She glanced down quickly and said, 'Oh no. He is very kind, you know, but I thought, "Perhaps this one time" – !'

Mee giggled and Myra, still looking down, giggled too.

('So that's another one of the Baddies taken care of,' thought Train. 'No Arthur Sonning. She's giving herself a rest from him. If she really were planning some sinister plot, Arthur Sonning would be in it.')

Train felt cheerful. He felt still more cheerful when he thought about Antigrav and the Smarties tube. Nobody knew where it was except Mee and himself. The tube was safe as houses. It was tucked into a gap in the lining of his sleeping bag.

And Pog's red stone?

'Ah-ha!' thought Train, 'once more the Baddies are foiled!' For Pog's stone was, all day, with Pog. At night, the stone was ceremonially removed from

Pog's bathing trunks, and placed first in a screw-topped jar that had once held Alka-Seltzer; then in a little coffee jar with a lid; then in his mother's handbag; and then under his mother's pillow. During this nightly security operation, Pog stood stoutly by, checking every detail. It was he himself who put the handbag under the pillow – stood back – and announced, 'All right now!'

And Pog and his mother were not going to Luish.

Myra said, 'You are not listening, Train, I think!' and laughed. He said, 'Sorry. What did you say?'

'Myra says, "Is there anything special you want to take?" ' said Mee. 'I'm taking my camera. Do you want to take yours? Do we need two?'

'No, just yours. Is Leo Alexander taking his binoculars?'

Myra said, 'His binoculars?' as if she was not clear of the meaning of the word. But then she said, 'Oh, yes. I am sure he will take those. I will ask him to do so.'

She got up and stretched. Train studied her and thought, 'If you had a glamour-puss face, you could be a beauty queen or something. But you have a soft, gentle, peasant-y face . . . a thinking face. Nice, trustworthy.'

In the distance, the other children were shouting again, singing some TV jingle deliberately out of tune. Myra said, 'Yes, we keep our little trip to ourselves, I think!' and laughed. She waved and walked away. She turned back and said, 'You will wake up? We start very early tomorrow, you know. Six in the morning. The boat goes at seven.'

'We'll be there!' said Mee and Train.

*

The voice said, 'Hey! Hey! Come on! Do wake up! Hey!' and Train woke up, pushing away the stick that kept prodding his ribs. He heard Mee laugh and saw the stick withdraw from underneath the edge of the tent. He said, 'All right, all right! I'm awake!' and looked at his wristwatch. Six-twenty. Forty minutes to get ready, eat something and join the others on the beach. He unzipped his sleeping bag, got up, put on his battered jeans and nothing else, and went outside.

'Gosh!' he said, 'it's freezing cold!'

Mee said, 'Then put some clothes on, stupid! Anyhow, it's going to be a scorcher. Look at the sky!'

Train squinted at the light and said 'Ugh.' Mee handed him a mug of coffee and Train said, 'I could have slept another whole twenty minutes if you hadn't come poking at me with that stick . . . You're right, it's going to be another hot day. Did you cook anything?'

'Only the coffee. Cold bangers, though. I've saved you three.'

He ate sausages, feeling better with each mouthful and said, 'Got all your gear?' She nodded at a pile of things. He said, 'There's enough there for a week in a luxury hotel!', but she took no notice and cheerfully poured more coffee. 'Drink up,' she said. 'The walk will take us a quarter of an hour. Ready?'

'OK, I'll just check up on Dad.' He went back into the tent and noticed for the first time that his father's sleeping bag was empty. He was not surprised – his father often got up at dawn – but asked Mee, 'Did you make the coffee, or was it Dad?' 'I made it,' said Mee. 'Has he gone on ahead?'

'I suppose so. Quick march?'

'Quick march,' replied Mee. They picked up their things and Mee began quietly to sing their marching song which repeated the same tune but never the same words after the first two lines.

> *'Om pom tiddle om, om pom tiddle om,*
> *Hear the banjos strumming,'* she sang.

> *'Can't think of a thing to say –*
> *Shame that Leo's coming,'* replied Train.

> *'Om pom tiddle om, I don't care,*
> *The weather will be glorious.'*

> *'You shouldn't leave me rhymes like that,'*
> Train replied,
> *'It makes me simply fuorious.'*

'That's cheating,' Mee said. The sun rose higher. The now-familiar landmarks – the Old Woman rock, the Army Tank boulder, the big hole they called the Moon Crater – seemed to focus themselves sharply in the brilliant early light.

Train said, 'What do you mean, cheating? Who's cheating? Hey! Look! There's the boat!'

They began the scramble down the rocks to the shore. The boat, cluttered with little figures, wavered luxuriously in the bright water. 'Posh!' said Train. And it was posh. White, rakish, with twin outboard motors towering above the stern. Train and Mee stopped to look at it, then turned to look at each other.

'Is that the "small boat" Myra was talking about?' said Mee. 'Because if it is, I wonder what she thinks a big boat looks like?'

Train said, 'That boat could hold everyone on our island and most of their luggage too. I wonder what she's up to – '

But at that moment, Myra herself saw them and came running up the rocks like an athlete. She grabbed Mee's baggage and cried, 'Is this not exciting? Such a boat! So big and splendid! Not at all like I am expecting! Hurry! Into the dinghy! Let us get on board!'

Mee and Train found themselves smiling at her, and then at each other – and then at the boat, as they boarded her. 'Help me with the anchor' Myra cried, waving them forward. 'We are allowed to be the sailors, you know? Come and help me!'

She fed the anchor chain, hollowly rattling, into the chain locker below and Mee and Train helped her, working fast and hard like Myra. There was a coughing *vrompf!* from one outboard motor, then the other, followed by a contented, powerful burbling. The anchor chain suddenly became heavy and the anchor itself appeared. They got it aboard – 'The paint! Oh, be careful of the paint!' shouted Myra as they swung it in – and beamed at each other, a good job well done.

The shore of the island spun – no, it was the nose of the boat, turning fast! – and the burbling of the motors became a low, capable, urgent growl. Suddenly there was a thrusting beneath their feet, sharp enough to make them catch their balance – the bows rose – the motors barked – the boat made a tiger leap for the open sea, hunched its broad shoulders and drove ahead, faster and faster, smashing down the waves, charging through them and over them, sending up cascades of jewelled spray.

Myra was laughing and clutching Mee. Spray glittered in their hair, wind tugged at their clothes. Train squatted alone in the bows, arms locked round his knees, in silent ecstasy. 'Oh yes!' he murmured, licking his salt-wet lips. 'Oh, yes!'

*

After a while, Mee sat beside him. They said nothing: there was nothing words could say. Every thought and sense belonged to the bold curve of the white bows, the arrogant surge forward, the innocent waves rushing towards them to be pounded into droplets and mist, the pouncing greed of the boat for ever more waves to be shattered into ever more rainbows . . .

Yet for Train, something was missing. What?

His father. Unwillingly, Train put his mind into an everyday gear and thought, 'He should be seeing this. I ought to go and get him.'

He got up, shouted 'Going to get Dad' into Mee's ear, and made his way aft. Myra smiled as he passed her. Czeslaw, mountainous in a folding canvas chair, lifted one finger. Train went into the cabin.

There were two men dressed like sailors; Leo, dressed like an advertisement in a glossy magazine; Arthur Sonning; and no one else.

Train turned back, confused. Why Arthur Sonning? Arthur Sonning was not supposed to be on this trip. And where was his father?

Suddenly the thought struck him – 'Where *could* he be?' Was there anywhere else on this boat? Yes, of course. The toilet. Without looking at Arthur, he pushed his way past and found himself in a small cabin – then at the very front of the boat, where the chain locker and the toilet had to be. He reached the toilet door. It was open, swinging on its hinges. Train knew the truth. His father wasn't anywhere on the boat.

He went aft again and confronted Leo. Before he could speak, Leo said, 'Hallo, Train. Thought you'd cut me dead. Gorgeous boat, isn't she? Now, if I liked boats, this is the sort of boat I'd like.'

Train said, 'Where's my father?'

'Twin Mercury motors!' said Leo, pointing aft. 'The driving force of a thousand horse, Train. Well, probably hundreds, anyhow. Is the girl friend all right? Mee, I mean?'

Train turned to Arthur Sonning and said, 'Where's my father?'

Arthur said, 'On the island, obviously. Didn't you get his note?'

'What note?'

'He left a note on your sleeping bag. Didn't you get it?'

'No. What did it say?'

'Well, I can hardly tell you that, the note wasn't addressed to me. But it must have been to the effect that he decided to stay and I decided to come.'

'But – why would he stay behind?' Train said.

Leo grinned, rather nastily. 'Your guess is as good as mine, son.'

Train felt a light hand on his shoulder: Myra. She said, 'I can think of a good reason, Leo!' Train understood: his father had stayed on the island to be alone with Peg. Train felt relieved and glad. His father and Peg together . . . bad luck, Leo!

Myra said, 'We are to go to the cabin. There are drinks, I think. Will you come?'

They went to the main cabin. Luish was very near now, Train noticed. Mee only glanced at Luish. Her lower lip was sticking out.

They were in the cabin. A sailor stood by the door, politely but unsmilingly holding it open. Two more sailors stood at the other side of the entrance, standing not at attention but not at ease either.

'Posh uniforms,' muttered Train.

'*Uniforms?*' Mee said, and swung her head to

look at Train, eyes wide, lips parted, suddenly alarmed and astonished. Train stared back at her. Inside him something like a lift rocketed down, its cables snapped; and landed with a sick thump in the pit of his stomach. 'Uniforms!' he said.

The sailors closed the doors. Everyone was in. People sat down. A sailor carried round a tray with drinks on it. And, looking enormous against the low ceiling, Czeslaw stood up.

'Welcome,' he said, blankly. 'You all have drinks? Good. And now I have welcomed you. So we can talk seriously.' He lifted a tiny glass and threw the colourless liquid in it down his throat, like spitting in reverse.

'That is Luish,' he said, nodding at a porthole. Heads turned to look. The grey and brown rockfaces of Luish were sliding past in the near distance. As they watched, the little scene ended: the boat was past the island, they were looking at nothingness of sky and sea.

'Always wanted to see Luish,' said Arthur Sonning, grinning. 'Ha ha.' Nobody took any notice of him. They were looking at their drinks, seeing a little close-knit pattern of ripples forming from the increased vibration of the motors. The motors had been opened up, the boat was going faster than ever. The little waves were being smashed by the bows in a regular, accelerating rhythm.

Train, half-standing, blurted, 'We were supposed to be going to Luish. Myra said we were going to Luish . . .' He looked at Myra. She looked away. Train sat down again and Mee took his hand. He looked at Leo, who managed a waxy grin. At Arthur, who stared straight back at him, sneering. At the sailor, who expressionlessly refilled his glass with lime juice, then two cubes of ice, then soda water. And last, at Czeslaw. Czeslaw, rock-faced and dead-eyed, looked back at him – no, through him – and automatically scratched his great thigh with a blunt, almost nailless finger.

Mee said, 'Take us back!' and rushed for the door. She flailed at it with her fists, screaming. The two sailors outside did not even turn to look at her, they just leaned their broad backs against the doors. The sailor in the cabin, the one with the drinks, unhurriedly put down his tray, went over to Mee, said 'Pliss!' and scooped her up in his arms. She beat at his leathery brown face but he did not seem to notice. He put her down beside Train – 'Pliss. Zank you.'

Czeslaw said, 'Very well. We talk business now. When the business is done, everything is OK, we all go home. But the business is very serious, it must be done, there can be no nonsense. Mr Sonning!'

Arthur got up, faced Train and Mee and said, 'You've got something Mr Czeslaw wants, you two have. So don't mess about. Hand it over.' He was grinning, as if he was enjoying himself. Train could see that he was the only one who was. Leo looked embarrassed. He kept taking sips of his drink, and turning the glass this way and that.

Mee shouted, 'You did it Leo! You and your binoculars, spying on us!' Arthur said, 'Never mind all that, we want those pebbles and a demonstration of what you do with them, right? Right. And smartish.'

'You won't get them,' said Train. 'I haven't got them. And if I had got them, I wouldn't give them to you. Any of you!'

'Oh yes you would, you know,' said Arthur, leaning over them. Mee tried to smack his face and missed. Arthur jumped back, startled.

Czeslaw waved his broad hand to and fro in front of his face and said 'Enough, enough.' He reached behind him, grunting, and pulled open a drawer in the fitted wall cabinet. He groped in the drawer and produced a big biscuit tin with a picture of roses on its lid. He prised off the lid with both thumbs and spilled the contents of the tin on the table in front of them.

Black stones.

There was complete silence as Czeslaw unhurriedly started filling an aluminium cigar tube with black stones. His big fingers were slow but not clumsy. He stopped when the tube was almost full: stood in front of Mee and Train; held the tube under their noses and said, 'I fill the tube but something is missing. Give me the missing thing to fill the tube and we all go home.'

'I don't know what you're talking about,' Train mumbled.

'But you do. I am talking about the red stone. Put it in the tube.'

'I told you, I haven't got a red stone. And if I had – '

'Turn out your pockets.'

Train turned out his pockets. Czeslaw said, 'Myra! Search the girl.'

Shamefaced, Myra began poking her fingers into Mee's clothing. Train stood foolishly with his pocket linings sticking out from his trousers. Arthur Sonning said, 'This is a stupid waste of time, strip them!' Czeslaw nodded and said, 'All the clothes off, please.'

Train said, 'I won't! You can't make me!' Czeslaw muttered something to the drinks sailor, and suddenly Train was upside down and his clothes were being pulled from his body. Arthur was trying to do the same thing to Mee. Train could see Mee's legs writhing and yelled, 'Leave her alone! Don't you touch her!' but it was no good. Then he was on his feet and right way up again, naked. He saw Arthur Sonning push Myra aside – heard him say, 'Oh, get *on* with it!' – and then the sailor pulled at Mee's clothes and she was naked too. Her clothes were in a mess round her ankles and Arthur was scrabbling at them with his fingers, poking into every seam. Mee was crying in gulping sobs.

Train kept his eyes away from Mee and glared at Czeslaw. 'You're a pig,' he said. 'You're all pigs, the whole lot of you!' He stared from face to face: at Myra, with a pulse in her throat jumping; at Leo, with a hangdog grin on his face, who kept his eyes away from Train's and topped up his drink; at

Arthur Sonning, busily grovelling on the floor, red-faced yet pleased with himself; and again at Czeslaw, who stared back at him with eyes like stones.

Czeslaw said, 'I want the red stone. Tell me where it is. Quickly.'

Train said, 'I haven't got it. *I haven't got it.* Can't you get that through your ugly head?'

'If you do not have it,' Czeslaw said. 'Where is it?'

'On the island!' screamed Mee, her face twisted with fury. 'It's not here at all! – do you think we're stupid? – it's on the island, where you can't get at it! It's safe! It's hidden away!'

Then she stopped, with her hand to her mouth. She had said too much.

Arthur chuckled and said, 'Hidden it, have you? Which proves you know it's valuable. Very valuable.'

Train said, 'You're not going to get it, at any rate.' Arthur put on his tough face. 'Listen, sonny, don't you tell me what – '

Czeslaw interrupted and Arthur immediately shut up. He said, 'It is a pity you do not have the stone. It wastes my time. But there is always more time . . .' He picked up a telephone and spoke words Train and Mee did not understand. Then he said, 'Another hour and a half and they will come. So. We must wait. Take the children away.' He began to scratch his thigh. His stony eyes looked at nothing.

*

An hour and a half later, the motors suddenly died and the boat went slack, wobbling in the ocean then heaving rhythmically as the waves rocked her.

Train said, 'Now what?' and looked out of the porthole of the little, neat cabin in which they were locked. Through the cabin door's porthole they could see the grainy leather neck of the drinks sailor.

Mee said, 'What's happening? Can you see anything?'

'Not a thing. Just sea and sky. Are you really all right now?'

She said, 'Yes, of course. Don't keep asking me, don't be so polite. What's happening? Let me have a look . . .'

He made room for her. Outside, the sea placidly made regular waves, each one sparkling its little crest in the sun. The sea seemed to go on forever. There was nothing else to look at.

Then Arthur came in.

'You'd better stop messing about, you two,' he said. 'We want that stone and we're going to get it.'

'Why do you want it? What's so marvellous about it?' said Train.

'Oh, come *on*, don't play dumb with *me*!' Arthur sneered. '*You* know what's what. You know what the stone means!'

'But I don't!' Train said. And Mee said, 'It was just a game . . . We put the red stone in with the black ones, and they sort of lifted . . .'

'Oh, come on, come *on*! You know what it means, I know what it means – '

'Then *tell* us!' said Train.

'Don't shout at me, Sunny Jim,' said Arthur. 'And don't come the innocent. That red stone means power, real power. A whole new world of power!'

'But what sort of power?' Train insisted. 'Power to do what? What's the good of it all? It's just a silly trick!'

'You think that, do you?' said Arthur, nodding his head consideringly. 'That's all you see in it? You've not got a lot of imagination have you? You're not exactly a bright pair of kids, are you?'

'I never said I was bright,' said Mee, very humbly and prettily, 'But I know that *you* are, and I wish you'd explain.'

Arthur seemed to expand and grow taller. He leaned close to Train and Mee and said, keeping his voice very low, 'Look. Imagine a nation with unlimited free power. No bother about coal and oil and nuclear reactors, all the power you can want – '

'I'm not that dim!' said Train, indignantly. 'Even I can understand about the power thing! It's obvious!'

'Oh yes, I understand that bit of it!' said Mee, turning her earnest, worried face to Arthur. 'But there must be something more . . . mustn't there? Something we wouldn't understand about. I mean, we're not clever, like – well, like you.'

Arthur's eyes darted from side to side. Then he said, conspiratorially, 'Space. *Weapons* in space. *Weapons* floating around in space, ready to be triggered off by a signal from earth – '

'But that's happened already!' said Train, looking disappointed. 'They send the space-thing, the weapon carrier, into orbit; and it just stays up there in space, waiting to be given radio instructions, like you said! I mean, it's been *done*!'

'But at what cost?' said Arthur, dramatically. At what cost in energy, human endeavour, technical resources? You kids simply can't imagine – well, I suppose it's reasonable, you are only kids – how difficult these things are. You can't imagine the problems involved in, say, applying the right amount of power to the weapon carrier . . . in keeping it in a *steady* orbit . . . endless complications! But if someone comes up with a simple, self-propelling, self-correcting power source – '

'You mean – our pebble?' breathed Mee.

'That's right! Your pebble! Look what it means! No energy needed for the launch! Automatic stability because the gravitational push-and-pull is something you compute beforehand, actually *measure* beforehand! No complex machinery to monitor and navigate and control the weapon-carrier – and dirt cheap! *Dirt cheap*! You don't have to think in terms of just one or two weapons, you can launch them in tens – hundreds – thousands!'

'What for?' said Mee, no longer girlish.

'What for?' said Arthur. 'What do you mean, what for? It's obvious, isn't it? To control the world, that's what for! To make the world do . . .'

'Do what?' said Mee.

'. . . Well, the right things!' said Arthur. 'Make it behave itself, obey orders. Make it peaceful.'

'Whose orders?' said Mee. 'Yours?'

'*You bloody kids*!' said Arthur – and left.

Mee looked at Train. Train looked at Mee. '*His* orders,' said Train at last. 'The orders of people like him! What a prospect!'

'Czeslaw's orders,' said Mee. 'Even worse. Orders from – from – oh, I don't know what. *Inhuman* people. Lots of men like Czeslaw . . . a whole gang of them, telling you and me and all the rest of us what to do.'

'And with the weapons, up there somewhere, to make sure we do it!' said Train. 'Do you know what I think? Whatever happens – however bad – we mustn't let them get Pog's pebble. We just mustn't, Mee!'

'No, we mustn't . . . But when they really get started on us, we might – '

'We mustn't!' said Train, firmly. 'Promise each other, Mee?'

'I promise,' she said, holding out her hand.

'I promise too.'

They shook hands.

*

Mee looked out of the porthole of their little cabin again. 'Anything happening?' Train asked.

'Nothing at all,' she said. 'So why have we stopped?'

'Let me look now,' said Train. Nothing. And

then – something: a pointed stick standing bolt upright in the water. 'Look!'

They shared the porthole. The stick grew longer. The water heaved, the pattern of the waves was broken. The water became smooth with little outward-going ripples at the edges of the calm area –

Then, shockingly, the water parted and from it, rising like a great building, there arose a shining, black, slab-sided tower. And then the great tower was dwarfed by the thing it stood on, a vast curved platform.

'Submarine!' Train whispered.

The cabin door banged open and the drinks sailor stood behind them, tapping their shoulders. 'Pliss,' he said, jerking his head towards the door. They followed him. 'Zank you,' he said, and led them to the dinghy that took them to the submarine.

*

Inside the submarine there was a continuous background hum of motors. They were led through rooms filled with tubes and consoles and controls and electronic displays; through bare corridors, walled with what looked like Formica; through big oval bulkheads with doors like the doors of bank safes; through a compartment with sailors in it, who stood to attention as they entered (except for two with padded headphones on, who never took their eyes from the displays facing them); along another short, bare, bright corridor; and so into a comfortable, ugly cabin, with curtains covering storage spaces in the walls.

'Flowered curtains . . . !' said Mee. Czeslaw heard her and, for the first time Mee and Train could remember, smiled. He poked a curtain with his big forefinger and said 'Modern'. Then, his face slab-like again, he sat down and nodded at the chairs round the central table. Everyone sat down. Czeslaw muttered orders to the drinks sailor, who went out.

When he returned, Czeslaw said, 'Good. There' and the sailor threw on the table a big canvas parcel tied with nylon rope. Czeslaw grunted and waved his hand: the sailor unlashed the parcel and threw open the canvas.

Inside, there was every possession that Train, Mee and their parents had brought to the island.

Train heard Mee catch her breath and give a little moan. He understood why. Their things looked so friendly yet so forlorn. There was the Primus stove, the shaft of its pump still shiny from hard use. There were the cooking things, Mee's brush and comb, a T-shirt that needed washing, a battered pocket chess set belonging to Train's father, a pair of sneakers with the sand of the island still trapped in the welts. Looking at these things gave Train the same feeling he had when he was stripped.

But then a worse thought struck him. 'What have you done to them? – our parents?'

'Nothing,' said Czeslaw.

'You have!' cried Mee. 'You've killed them or taken them away! You've – '

'Oh, belt up and use your brains!' Arthur sneered. 'What do we care about your parents? What can they do to hurt us? Why should we bother to hurt them? We don't need them!'

Czeslaw waved him down and said, in his blank flat, immovable voice, 'We need the red stone. That is all. It is here. Where?' He pointed at the litter of possessions on the table.

'It's not anywhere in that lot!' said Train. 'So now what?'

'It is there,' said Czeslaw. 'The little boy liked the stone. He kept it always safe. Show me where. In this?' He picked up Mee's toilet bag and, expressionlessly, ripped it apart with two fingers. Her toothbrush, face flannel, nailbrush and toothpaste fell on the table. Czeslaw said, 'So. Not in the bag. This?'

And as Mee and Train watched, things were split, ripped, torn and pulled apart. Czeslaw came to Pog's bathing trunks. His blunt fingers entered the pocket; pulled; stitches ripped, the torn pocket flapped; the trunks, absurdly small and cheerful, were thrown aside. Mee began to cry.

Train concentrated on not looking at Mee's mother's handbag. There was a bulge in the handbag and Train knew that the bulge was made by a little coffee jar with a lid, that contained an Alka-Seltzer jar, which contained Pog's red pebble . . .

Inevitably, Czeslaw came to the handbag. 'Ah,' he muttered, and ripped the bag apart. Mee said, 'You dirty pig! That's my mother's!' and Arthur

Sonning leaned over the table and hit her in the face with his open hand. She gasped and stared at him, amazed.

'We mean business, kiddy!' said Arthur.

Czeslaw nodded at the drinks sailor and murmured something. The sailor strode to Arthur, put his hands on Arthur's shoulders and sat him down hard.

For a moment, Train felt grateful to Czeslaw. But then Czeslaw spoke to Mee, leaning forward to bring his face closer to hers. He said, 'You are a *silly - little - girl*, yes? So. It is easy to hurt you very badly and make you scream and cry out. Then you do the things you are told, do you understand?' She seemed hypnotized by his slow, careful words. Czeslaw continued, 'I do not mean the face slap, that is nothing. I mean *bad* things, very bad things, things that last for always. Now, do you understand me? Do you?'

She said nothing and began to tremble. She could not hide the trembling and hid her face in her hands.

Train felt a numbing coldness inside him. He was so cold and clear inside that he was able to think. He watched Czeslaw without hate, without anger, as the man unscrewed the little coffee jar's lid and took out the Alka-Seltzer tube. He watched the big fingers loosen the cap of this tube. His cold, clear mind said, 'Wait! Another turn!' – and then, when the cap was just about to come off, he acted.

'You stupid little cow!' Train yelled and flung

himself at Mee, flailing at her with his hands ('No need to hit her head,' said his cold, clear mind). She looked up at him, horrified, but he continued to beat at her ('That was a good loud smack, when you hit her shoulder!' said his mind) until she stood up and backed away from him. The sailor moved towards him but Czeslaw stopped this interference ('Good!' said Train's mind) and he kept on at her, driving her back, cursing her. 'You gave it away!' he yelled, between blows. 'You spoiled everything, on the boat! You told them the stone was on the island and now they've got it!' ('Get her nearer the table!' said his mind, 'Then give her a good shove! That's right! Push!')

He pushed at her and she sprawled across the table, her body covering that Alka-Seltzer tube. He bent over her, still hitting her with his right hand. ('Careful!' said his mind, 'You're nearly there! Keep your face furious – and keep yelling!') His left hand propped him up and found the Alka-Seltzer tube. His thumb levered off the cap. He felt the cold smooth stone – clutched it in his fist – and ('Use your clenched fists now, not your open hands!' said his mind) started beating at Mee with his fists, making wide swings that landed but did not hurt.

'Enough!' said Czeslaw – and the drinks sailor picked Train up, still punching and shouting, and twisted his left arm up behind his back until the pain silenced him. ('Very nice!' said his mind, 'very nice indeed!')

Czeslaw said, 'No more stupid nonsense. An arm

can be broken. You are a sensible boy. Tell me where is the red stone.' He said something else in his own language, and the sailor half-released Train's arm. ('Fine!' said his mind; 'Now you can stand up very straight, lower lip sticking out and *both fists tightly clenched*. And then you can "confess" everything!')

Train said, 'If I tell you, will you let me go?'

Czeslaw said, 'Yes. Immediately. You will be taken back to the island. The girl too.'

'I don't care about *her*,' said Train, sneering. Mee looked up at him. ('Take no notice of that look,' said his mind. 'Don't be sorry for her. Stick to the point!')

'The red stone,' said Czeslaw.

'You've got it!' Train replied; and coolly sat down on the red leathercloth divan running round two sides of the room ('Slip the stone down, between the cushion and the backrest!' said his mind. 'That's it! That's right!'). 'You've got the stone! You'd just come to it when I lost my temper with this stupid little idiot! The stone is in that Alka-Seltzer jar!'

Mee cried, 'Oh! Oh, how *could* you! How *could* you tell them!' and wept in utter despair. Czeslaw picked up the Alka-Seltzer tube, looked inside; and looked again. 'In this?' he said, holding the empty tube out to Train. 'But it is empty – !'

'Empty?' said Train. He jerked to his feet. 'That's impossible! – ' And Mee looked up, her wet eyes startled. 'It's *got* to be there in the tube!' Train said. 'It's always put there, every night! Ask her!' And he hurried to help Czeslaw search for the stone, impatiently picking through the jumble of articles on the table. He even looked on the floor, with the sailor and Leo helping, while Arthur Sonning made Mee tell every detail of the nightly ritual of putting the stone away safely.

*

'Very well,' said Czeslaw ten minutes later. 'The stone is not there. We have not got it and that is a pity.'

'But it's – it's *impossible*!' said Train, lamely. 'That's the only place it could have been! I mean, I *saw* the stone put in that jar last night! And *your* people took the handbag and the handbag had the stone in it, so it must be somewhere!'

'Take them to their cabin,' said Czeslaw. And Arthur Sonning and Myra took them away.

Locked up in the cabin with Mee, Train's mind collapsed in a wet heap. 'Tell Mee!' it urged him. 'Tell her you're still on her side! – you only pretended to be a traitor – you had to hit her! Tell her all that, and perhaps she'll look at you, and not just sit there hating you!'

But then Train told his mind to shut up. Things were only just beginning. Czeslaw wouldn't give up, he'd keep the pressure on. It was good that Mee didn't know the truth – good, because whatever was done to her, she could not tell what she did not know. She did not know the stone was safely hidden. Train knew, she didn't. Good.

'But she hates you,' his mind said. 'How long can you stand that?' He did not have to answer the question. The door opened and Arthur came in. When he left, Myra entered. When she left, Arthur returned.

The girl would come in looking pretty and wholesome and sincere and anxious for them. She seemed always on the verge of sympathetic tears.

Arthur remained imitation-tough, bullying, sweating. Train could see from his jerky movements and the way his voice got higher and higher as he raged at them, that he was on the edge of violence.

Arthur: 'Oh yes, you're such clever kids, aren't you? Smart, that's what you think you are! Well, think again! You're up against some *really* smart people! – smart, and if necessary, nasty! You heard what Czeslaw said, Mee! He said he'd hurt you, right? He doesn't say things like that for fun, you know. Oh, no, not for fun. Not Czeslaw!

'And you, Train! You're the boy wonder, aren't you? That's what you're thinking, isn't it? You know where the red stone is and you're not going to tell. Well, let *me* tell *you* something. You *are* going to tell. You'll be begging me to be allowed to tell! You'll be grovelling on your hands and knees to tell! Not because of me, oh no, I'm a nice enough person, I don't want to bruise my knuckles on you. But there's men on this boat, sonny, ready and willing to–

'Hey, are you listening to me? Are you? Listen, sonny, when I talk to you! Listen! Attend! Look me in the eye, get it?'

(Train thought, 'He's hurting me, digging his fingers into my jaw like that and pulling my head about. Now he's going to hit me. There! He's hit me. Now another one, with the back of his hand. As long as he doesn't hit poor old Mee. I wish I could explain to Mee, she looks awful, she looks so sad. Is he going to hit me again? No, because it would mark my face. What a stupid face he's got, what a mean little man, what a drip. But he's hurting me, that's a good thing, he'll think I'm crying. When he shouts like that, I get his spittle on my face; I hate that. I wish I could explain to Mee . . .')

Myra: 'These are very dangerous people, so dangerous . . . ! Oh, please! – why will you not tell them what they want to know? Why won't you? Can you not see what must happen to you? Surely you can see that? Surely you can see what they will do to you both? Why won't you see? Oh dear, it is such a stupid thing you do . . . this stupid little red stone, why must you be so stubborn? It is only a pebble and yet it could lead to the most horrible, the most terrible things for you! Things I have seen in another country, things I cannot speak about, things I try not to think about! And they will happen to you unless you do what they ask! Oh, *please*, Mee, do not let these dreadful things happen to you! It is so simple, so easy! . . . *Please* . . . !'

(Mee thought, 'Train and I promised each other. We swore an oath and he broke it. How could he? I wish Myra would stop. That pretty voice with the pretty accent going on and on . . . I wonder if she is really sorry for us? She keeps pretending she wants to save us from this and protect us from that, I wonder if she means it? I suppose you can make yourself mean something if you say it often enough. And then Train hit me, he hit me again and again as if he'd gone mad. Mad with cowardice! He's such a coward that he'd do anything at all . . . the way he grovelled on the floor, trying to find Pog's stone . . . Poor Pog, what is he doing now? What are they all doing? I wonder if I would tell Myra where the stone is, if I knew? But I don't know, I don't understand anything, it should have been in the Alka-Seltzer tube . . .')

Myra stopped. Arthur took over. Arthur stopped, Myra took over.

Myra said, 'We cannot go on like this much longer, you know. Czeslaw will not allow it, don't you see? He wants us to persuade you to tell, without – without *hurting* you. But you will not listen! I do not know how I can help you, you will not let me help you! You do not seem to understand the position you are in, you do not seem to think of your poor parents – '

'What about our poor parents?' Train interrupted. 'You've stolen us, you've stolen all their things, do you think they're going to just sit there on that island and let it happen? Do you think – ?'

Arthur came in. 'I'll tell you what I think,

sonny,' he said, 'I think there's not one single solitary thing your parents can do! They're on that island and they can stay there – just sit there and let it happen, as you said! What do you expect them to do? Pick up the telephone and dial 999? Send a telegram? Smoke signals? Swim to the mainland? What do you think they're doing *right now* to help you? I'll tell you what *I* think they're doing. I think your mother, Mee, is crying her eyes out. And your father, Train, has got his manly, protective arm round her shoulders and he's saying, "Blah-blah, boo-hoo, it will be all right in the end". And a fat lot of good that does *you*. Because you're here, and I'm here and the red stone is here. Now, I've just spoken to Czeslaw and he's losing his patience . . .'

'What was that?' gasped Mee in sudden terror.

'What was what?' said Arthur, enjoying himself. 'Did you think you heard something? What did you think you heard?'

'There! That!' cried Mee. From a long way away, there was a high voice, shouting.

'Oh, *that*!' said Arthur, smiling like a crocodile. 'That's your little brother, Mee! Little Pog!'

'*Pog* . . . !'

'Yes, Pog. We sent out a little night mission – three sailors in a rubber dinghy with a big outboard motor – and they picked him up in the middle of the night. Nice surprise for your mother when she wakes up, Mee. Give her something else to worry about. A change is as good as a rest, right?'

'*Pog*!' screamed Mee and pressed her cheek to the door of the cabin, listening.

She heard the little high voice cry, 'Mee! Oh yes! I want you!' Then she heard the sound of Pog crying.

*

Czeslaw came in. Mee ran at him, hitting at him and screaming words that made nonsense. He just stood there, looking above her head and letting her hit him while he spoke to Train. Czeslaw said, 'Do you have the red stone?'

'No.'

'Do you know where is the red stone?'

'No, no, no, NO. And why did you have to bring Pog into this? He's only a baby.'

Czeslaw said to Mee, 'Do you want to see the little boy, your brother?' She said 'Yes'. Czeslaw jerked his head and the drinks sailor, standing in the doorway, went away. He came back with Pog. Mee snatched him into her arms and hugged him. He said, 'Crying!' and began to cry himself. 'I'm crying too,' he said, 'Look!' And he pointed at the tears on his face.

Czeslaw said, 'There. You have your little brother. He is safe and well. You must keep him so, is that right?'

Mee said 'Yes. Yes, anything . . . !'

'I do not want *anything*, I want the red stone. Do you have it?'

'I told you – no!'

'Do you know where it is?'

'You asked me that, I told you – '

'Do you love this little brother of yours?'

Mee said nothing: she clasped Pog to her. He said, 'Pog's stone! Where is it? My red stone!' and looked accusingly at Train, and Myra and Czeslaw and the sailor.

Czeslaw said, 'So. You have your little brother, I do not have the red stone. That is a bad bargain for me, you understand? A *bad bargain*.' He seemed pleased with the phrase. Train saw his thick lips move as he mouthed the words 'bad bargain' for the third time. Then he said, 'I leave you together now so that you may discuss. Later on, I will come back and I will make you separated, you understand? Not together any more.'

'Pog . . . !' said Mee. 'You can't do that, you can't leave him all alone – '

Myra said, 'Oh, think of the child! Think of your parents! Think of them! Do what he says, give him what he wants! If you do not obey him, bad things will happen – ' She burst into tears.

Czeslaw said, 'The little brother likes toys? He likes to play?'

Mee whispered, 'Yes.'

'Then I give him a toy!' said Czeslaw, his high voice thickening with what could have been anger, frustration, scorn, anything at all. From the pocket of his linen jacket he pulled a handful of the black stones and threw them, like a farmhand feeding chickens, on the ground before Pog. 'Toys!' said Czeslaw, louder: another handful from another pocket. 'Toys!' he shouted and dug in his pockets for handfuls of stones.

Then, his voice very quiet, he said, 'You play games with your toys. Good. You play games with Czeslaw. Bad. I give you the stones I have, worthless toys. You give me the pretty red stone – the game is then finished, it is over, we are all friends, all safe, nobody is hurt.'

'My stone,' said Pog. 'My *red* stone . . . ?' He looked up questioningly.

'You had better answer him,' said Czeslaw, heavily. 'Now I have things to do. I give you an hour. One hour.' The door slammed behind him. Mee, Train and Pog were alone.

*

Pog gently patted Mee's cheeks and said, 'No crying any more. Over now.' She said, 'Oh yes! All right now, darling Pog, oh, darling Pog! Were the men nice to you? Did they hurt you?'

'On a boat I was,' said Pog. He made motor-boat noises, staring earnestly at Mee to see if she understood him. 'All rubber it was. With sailors . . .'

'What did Mummy say to the sailors?' said Mee, keeping her voice calm.

'She was sleeping in the night,' he said, and stuck.

'You mean, she was asleep when the sailors came?'

'Yes,' said Pog. 'There were sailors when she was asleep and I was asleep.'

'Did they carry you away?' said Mee.

'Oh yes. Away. Mummy didn't see, nobody didn't see. Away to the boat. It was all rubber and I was sleepy.'

'Were the sailors kind to you?' said Mee. She could not stop herself hugging Pog and touching him. He put up with this. Sometimes, dutifully, he patted her cheek or her hair.

'The rubber boat went *vroom*!' said Pog. 'Very fast, up and down in the water. All rubber. Special for Pog.'

'How was Mummy, Pog? Was she well?'

'She kept crying,' said Pog, matter-of-factly.

'Why did she cry?'

'She had a headache. So she cried.' Then Pog said, in a voice startlingly like his mother's, 'It's only a headache, I'm all right really.'

For the first time in hours, Mee looked at Train. She said, 'Is there anything you want to ask Pog?'

Train said, 'Pog, were there any new people on the island? People not there when we were all there?'

'The sailors,' said Pog.

'No, I don't mean the sailors. Were there any – any policemen, or soldiers, or people like that? Did people come to the island on boats?'

Pog thought and said, 'Oh no.' And then, again in his mother's voice, he said, 'We are cut off.'

'That's what your mother said?'

'Cut off,' said Pog, enjoying the words. 'She said that. And then she cried with the headache.'

Train said to Mee, 'So they're right. No help coming from the mainland for us or for them.'

Mee shook her head at him, meaning, 'Don't use words that Pog may understand. Disguise what you say.'

Train said, 'So our Friends here – OK? – needn't do anything they don't want to do. Because our Real Friends can't say anything to anyone. What worries me is what they mean to do to our smallest real friend. Do you really think they would hurt – ?'

'They'd do anything, anything at all, to get what they want. And we haven't got *it*, so we can't – '

'But we have!' said Train.

She stared at him, amazed. '*What* did you say?'

*

And he explained everything. Why he had attacked her; how he had got the red stone; how he had hidden the red stone in the cushions in the cabin; everything.

'And all the time I thought . . .' she said.

'I know what you thought. I'm sorry I did what I did and hit you, but I had to. We promised each other – '

'I'm not sorry at all. Oh, Train, and all this time I've been thinking – '

'It doesn't matter now, does it? Because our Friends here have won, haven't they? I mean, we promised each other not to – you know – but we can't make promises for our smallest friend.'

'But I can't believe they'd – '

'They will do it, they will. I know they will.

Think of the worst thing in the world and double it – they'll do that,' said Train, miserably.

'How long have we got left?' said Mee. 'Half an hour? Czeslaw said an hour. How long ago was that?'

Pog was making a heap of black stones in a corner. He said, 'Pog's red stone. *Gone*!' and stared at them accusingly. 'Don't worry, Pog, we'll find it,' Mee said. Then she stared at Train. While Pog's back was turned, she pointed at the black stones and said, in a hushed voice, 'He's got those and we've got *the other* . . . Perhaps if we – '

'I know. I've been thinking about it all the time. But what's the use? Anyhow, we haven't got ''the other'', we just know where it is. They wouldn't let us reach it and even if they did I don't see how it would help. Even if we had it, what the hell would we actually do with it?'

'The rubber boat,' said Mee: and made going-along wavy motions with one hand. 'Power to drive it!'

'You seem to forget we're about to be s-e-p-a-r-a-t-e-d,' Train spelt out. 'And also that we're I don't know how many feet under water.'

'But we're not! We are on the surface! The motor thing that makes the humming noise isn't on and I can *smell* the sea. Can you?'

Train sniffed and said, 'You're right! You're right!' Then his excitement died. 'All we'd have to do,' he continued, 'is to get past our Friends – not be noticed stealing the dinghy – not be chased – oh yes, and first of all we'd have to get *it* – and get all these black ones into the right sort of containers, firmly strapped to the dinghy because of the pull –'

'But couldn't we use the outboard on the dinghy?'

'Oh, sure. *If* we knew how to start it first go, without making a racket. *If* we knew how to make it run silently, so that the noise wouldn't wake everyone up in this tin fish. And *if* the tank is full of petrol, which it probably isn't.' He trailed off. Mee said, 'How long do you think we've got left now?'

'Minutes, I suppose.'

They were all three of them silent. Pog was staring fascinated at his left foot as if he had never seen it before. They sat there, thinking their own separate thoughts. The only sound was the soft hiss Train had noticed earlier.

Then there was a little noise like *DCK!* – and the hissing stopped.

Train leapt to his feet. The *DCK!* noise had come from there – no, there, behind a shelf with official looking books on it. He pushed the books to one side and saw a small grille. The grille was coarse. It was easy to see a bend of metal here and a screw head there that told him what lay behind the grille: a loudspeaker. And to one side of it – a small microphone.

'Mee!' he said, 'I think they've been listening to every word we've been saying!'

The door opened: the door slammed shut: and,

standing with his back against it was the massive figure of Czeslaw.

*

His broad face was as blank as ever.

'That's right,' he said. 'I listen, I hear, I understand everything you say. So.' There was no triumph in his voice, no self-congratulation. He was stating a fact.

Train made himself speak. 'All right,' he said, 'So it's all over. We were stupid, you were clever.'

'Now you needn't hurt – anyone,' said Mee, glancing at Pog and appealing to Czeslaw with her eyes.

'I find it in the red cushions, as you directed,' said Czeslaw, taking no notice of her. Keeping his hand high and cupped so that Pog could not see, he showed Train the little red pebble, Pog's stone.

'You must be very pleased and proud of yourselves,' said Mee, insultingly . . . But her voice trembled and in any case Czeslaw was not listening. He frowned and tossed the red pebble up and down, up and down, in his broad cupped hand.

'Rulers of the universe,' said Train, shakily. 'Hurrah for you. Weapons in the sky.'

'That is so,' said Czeslaw, not really listening. Train looked at Mee. Their looks said '?'

'A good bargain,' Czeslaw said at last. 'From this little thing' – he threw the red pebble – 'so much power . . .'

A voice outside the door, Arthur's voice, called, 'Mr Czeslaw? You in there?'

Czeslaw said, 'Yes. Go away.'

'But it's me, Mr Czeslaw. The hour's up – '

'That is so,' said Czeslaw. 'Go away.'

'All right, sir,' said Arthur's puzzled voice. 'I thought you'd want to know and I didn't know where you were – '

'Enough!' said Czeslaw. And then, once again speaking almost to himself, he said, 'Go away.'

They heard Arthur's footsteps retreating.

Mee said, 'You're going to let us go now, aren't you? Aren't you, Mr Czeslaw?'

'You don't need us any more,' Train said. 'You've got what you want so we can go home. Can't we?'

But Czeslaw had cupped his great hands together. Inside the hollow was the pebble. Czeslaw rocked his hands to the right and to the left, feeling the pebble touch this palm, that palm. 'Good bargain, bad bargain,' he said, 'Good bargain, bad bargain.'

'Mr Czeslaw – ' said Mee. She touched the rocking hands.

'There is an English word I cannot think of,' said Czeslaw. 'You shall help me find it.'

'Mr Czeslaw, it isn't fair!' said Mee. 'You can't keep us! I don't mind for me and Train, but he's got nothing to do with it! – ' She pointed at Pog. He was collecting all the black stones Czeslaw had flung on the floor.

'*Balance*!' cried Czeslaw. 'That is the word! Balance. You say in English "To strike a balance", is that not so?'

'Yes. But *please*, Mr Czeslaw – '

'The girl Myra is a good girl,' Czeslaw said, looking over Mee's head. He was still tossing the pebble back and forth in his cupped hands. 'She has seen bad things, the worst things, but she is still good. But she is also *weakened*.' He looked at Mee. 'You too are a good girl,' he told her, 'and you are too young to be weakened yet. So.'

'Please! You *must* let us go, you *can't* – '

'The man Arthur Sonning,' Czeslaw said – his eyes looking over Mee's head again – 'is *nothing*!' The word came out like an airgun going off. 'There are a million such in every nation. A nothing man . . .

'And the Doctor Alexander, he is a clever-silly. We have many of those too. To be clever is good, to be silly is bad. There must be a balance.'

Train burst out, 'You won't listen to us! You just go raving on, not listening to anybody! – '

Czeslaw cut him short by looking directly at him with round, pale eyes that chilled.

'Your father,' said Czeslaw, 'He seems a good man. And your mother,' he said, looking at Mee, 'I think she is a good woman. Is not that strange? I have command of people who are not very good, not good enough – and on the other side, I have people who seem not so bad. That is not balanced. So what should I do?'

'Just let us go, Mr Czeslaw!'

'But I cannot!' said Czeslaw, his high, loud voice suddenly revealing something human. 'I cannot be seen to fail! You can understand that?

Oh yes, I think you can. You are not stupid, you children, I have learned that. There are many things you do not know about the world . . . but you are not stupid. So even you can see that I cannot let you go!'

'But I *am* stupid, I *don't* see!' Train shouted.

'I do,' said Mee, quietly. 'I know what Mr Czeslaw means. He is afraid! There are other men, just like him only worse – '

'Mee!' Train warned. But Czeslaw said, 'No, let her speak. What are words to me? What do the words matter?'

'They seem to matter to you,' Mee pointed out, gently. 'A little while ago, you were thinking about words.'

Surprisingly, Czeslaw laughed. The ugly face became even uglier, yet more likeable. 'So!' he said. 'A clever girl! Now tell me what I was thinking when I said those words!'

Mee said, 'You were thinking about – about what you are holding in your hands. Thinking that when you gave that thing to the people above you, they would be pleased with you and that all kinds of things *they* want to happen, *could* happen. Power . . . you were thinking about that. Like being a king, an emperor, ruling the world.'

'*I* would not be that king,' said Czeslaw.

'No, but you would be the kingmaker. And things you believe in would happen. The world would run *your* way, the way you have always wanted. All because of that little thing you are holding. A good bargain! Isn't that right?'

Before Czeslaw could answer, Train said, 'But then you thought about the bad side of the bargain. You thought about Arthur Sonning and Leo and Myra –'

'Not about them,' said Czeslaw, impatiently. 'I do not think about such people. I thought about the men above me and what they might do with the power I give them. That is the bad bargain, perhaps?'

'Perhaps?' said Train. 'Why ''perhaps''? If they're not good men – if they're bad men, dangerous men – how can there be any ''perhaps''?'

Again, Czeslaw laughed. He said, 'Oh, I see! You are children after all, silly children! You believe that on your side it is all good, all the men are good men; and on my side it is all bad things, bad men! You think the power of this little thing –' he shook the pebble in his cupped hands ' – is safe with your mummy and daddy, but not so safe with the mummy and daddy of another country! Is that what you think?'

'But you said yourself,' Train said, 'that my father and her mother are good people –'

'I did not say they were *strong* people,' said Czeslaw. 'You are good children, nice children – but you are not *strong*. And I shall tell you this: the world is run by the *strong*!'

There was an iron chill about the word when Czeslaw said it. Even Pog caught the chill. 'St-h-rrong . . .' he said, worriedly, imitating Czeslaw. Then he said, 'Where's Mummy?'

Mee, her voice small and hopeless, said, 'What are you going to do about us?'

Train said, 'Can't you just throw it away and then let us go? If you don't trust our sort of people or your own people, why not just chuck the thing in the sea and –'

'That would be very nice,' said Czeslaw, 'But I would also have to throw in the sea all the people who *know*. Arthur Sonning, Leo Alexander, Myra – they all know and they would tell. The knowledge is power for them. And for me, their knowledge is – Crrrk!' He made an ugly noise in his throat.

'And then there's us,' said Train, shakily. 'You'd have to do away with us too.'

'But not Pog!' Mee said. 'You don't have to do anything to Pog?'

Czeslaw made no reply. He threw the red stone from palm to palm in his cupped hands.

Mee said, 'You can't hurt Pog!'

Czeslaw spoke at last. 'The world is not good,' he said, heavily. 'There are so many bad things . . . And this little stone: I ask myself, a good bargain or a bad bargain? I think it is a bad bargain. The world is not ready for such a thing. But then, *I* am not ready for disgrace and death. They would do bad things to me, to my wife . . .' He was silent again, his pale eyes staring unseeing over their heads.

Then Leo was outside the door. They heard him knock, and his determined voice saying, 'Czeslaw! It's Doctor Alexander. Have you any instructions for us?'

Czeslaw said nothing. Leo called, 'Czeslaw! Are you in there?'

Czeslaw pulled himself out of the depth of his thoughts and said, 'What do you want?'

'We want to know what's happening. Haven't you any instructions to give? Aren't we supposed to be *doing* something?'

Czeslaw said, 'Yes. I have instructions. Assemble everybody aboard in the stateroom.'

'Everybody? But why?'

'Everybody,' said Czeslaw.

'Even including the monitoring officers and crews? And the duty men? Do you mean them too? For God's sake, Czeslaw – '

'Everybody.'

They heard Leo go away and stared at Czeslaw's set face. 'What are you going to do?' said Train, huskily.

'Nothing,' said Czeslaw. 'I talk to the people in the stateroom. I keep talking. But *you* are going to do something.'

'I don't understand.' said Train. 'Do what?'

'That is up to you. The submarine is on the surface of the water. The sea is not rough. There is a rubber dinghy. I will lead you to where the dinghy is and you will not be seen, for everybody will be in the stateroom.'

'But then what happens?' said Mee.

'I do not know. You have escaped, that is all.'

'But what will you tell the others? What will you say?'

'I do not know. Come with me. Bring the little boy.'

Pog said, 'My stones!' and pointed to the wastepaper basket.

'Bring them too.'

*

He led them through the deserted submarine. He stopped at a small cabin, seized a pile of neatly folded blankets and thrust them into Train's arms. He stopped at the gleaming galley, the ship's kitchen, and selected a dozen tins of food which he packed in a square stainless steel basin. Mee said 'Opener' and Czeslaw grunted. The only opener was a fixture on the wall. He reached in his own pocket and found a heavy knife with many blades. He slipped the knife into Train's pocket and said, 'Come. Hurry.' He led them on through the ship – pausing once to pick up a hank of strong twine, which he thrust into Train's other pocket – until they reached the conning tower. Heavily, he climbed the ladder and opened the tower hatch. 'The little boy,' he said. Train carried Pog up the ladder. Czeslaw reached down, grabbed Pog's arm and effortlessly swung him up and over. 'Hurry,' was all he said. Train and Mee obeyed him as if in a dream, or nightmare.

Then they were standing on the very edge of the submarine's hull and the rubber dinghy was beneath them nudging the whale-like curve of the hull. 'Do not use the motor at first,' Czeslaw said. 'Use the oars. They are silent.'

'Is there any petrol in the motor?' Train asked.

'I do not know.'

'But it's miles to the island!'

'That is so. Many miles. You must steer to the west. Point the boat at the sun and keep the wind at your backs. It is an east wind, you understand. There is a little compass in the locker of the dinghy. Steer west. There are fishing boats, you may be seen.'

'But we don't know about boats, and quite soon it will be dark –'

'That is so,' said Czeslaw, blankly. 'You wish to stay?'

'No!'

'We'll go,' said Mee.

'Then go.'

They carefully put Pog into the dinghy, got in themselves and, dazed, watched Czeslaw unhitch and hold on to the dinghy's white nylon line. The dinghy bobbed and bounced against the side of the submarine. Czeslaw said, 'There is the locker. Open it. Good. Here are the black stones for the little boy.' He handed over the wastepaper basket. Pog, as dazed and silent as the others, quietly said, 'My stones' and clasped his arms round the basket.

'Here are the tins of food and the opener. You have the knife and the string. You have a compass and the blankets.'

Train, white-faced, said, 'But we can't –' and then shut up, unable to make sense of his own thoughts. Czeslaw replied, 'You cannot go without the red stone? Very well. Can you catch?'

'Yes, but – '

Czeslaw put his hand in his pocket; held up the red stone; and very carefully threw it. Train caught it. Pog said, 'Pog's stone! Red!' but Train held on to it.

'Now go,' said Czeslaw.

Mee shouted at him, her voice shaking and hysterical. 'We might die! You're a coward and a bully! You talk about people having to be strong, yet you do *this*!'

'That is so,' said Czeslaw. 'Now go.'

They watched his broad back, his short arms and legs, the pink-white baldness of his head, as he climbed the ladder. They heard him grunt as he threw his leg over the edge of the tower and glimpsed his face for the last time as it disappeared under the tower's edge.

'He didn't even look back at us,' said Mee.

Train said, 'Give me the other oar. You steer – get the compass out and make sure I keep going west.'

When he had rowed for ten minutes or so, the submarine was just a small black silhouette on the glinting waters.

*

Mee said, 'I'll row now' and they carefully clambered past each other as she reached for the oars.

They had been rowing, turn and turn about, for

what seemed to be hours. They had tried to start the outboard motor without success. And anyhow, there was very little petrol in the tank. Train watched Mee wrap her hands with strips torn from a blanket. The strips cushioned their blisters but made rowing a slippery business. He said, 'OK?' She said, 'Right. Set me on course.'

At first, they had found it difficult to keep a course. The rubber dinghy wallowed and tried to spin. Now they had got the knack. Train glanced constantly at the compass and nodded his head to left or right to correct Mee's rowing. On the whole, they were heading west.

Pog, full of tinned soup, slept. For Mee and Train, the numb, dreamlike feeling had gone. The sea was real, the pain of their blisters was real, the hope of being seen was real. They talked.

'I still don't see why he let us go,' said Mee. 'Just throwing us out in a small boat on an empty sea . . . Yet I don't think it was just cruelty or coldness or spite . . .'

'I think I see it now,' Train said. 'He kept raving on about "bad bargains" and "good bargains" and "striking a balance", didn't he? Well, there you are! In the end, he just left it to chance, like throwing a dice. He doesn't trust his own people, he doesn't trust our sort of people, he doesn't trust anyone – so he's just tossed for it by letting us go!'

'Funny way to solve the world's problems,' said Mee. 'Something really big comes up and tough powerful Czeslaw says "Leave it to the kids!" I think he's just a big, stupid, cowardly murderer.'

'He's probably been a murderer quite often in his life. And he's certainly big. But stupid? Cowardly? I mean, what *should* he have done?'

'I suppose he should have murdered *us*,' said Mee, thoughtfully.

She stopped rowing and adjusted the blanketing round her hands. 'They're hurting like mad,' she said. 'I don't know how long we can go on like this.' She began rowing again and said, 'Why didn't he just chuck the pebble in the sea? Why?'

'Perhaps that's the brave part,' said Train. 'Perhaps he believes that something really good can come out of the red stone, *if* the stone is put into the right hands. Perhaps he believes that our hands are the right hands.'

Mee thought about this during five or six strokes of the oars and then said, 'In a pig's eye! He's just not like that! He's not all noble and visionary and Trust The Little Children!' She rowed faster – then stopped.

'I've only just thought of it, it only just struck me . . . I mean, suppose everyone else on the submarine gangs up on Czeslaw and insists on chasing after us . . .'

'He got them all into the main stateroom,' Train interrupted. 'Leo thought it was fishy, do you remember? He couldn't believe Czeslaw meant it –'

'But Czeslaw wasn't the captain, was he?' Mee said. 'So suppose the real captain, the naval captain, overrides Czeslaw and says "Go and get the dinghy back"?' She started rowing, hard.

Train said, 'Perhaps we'd better stop fooling

around with the oars and begin using our loaves. Look, we've got lots of black stones, lots of tins, ropes and lines, that wastepaper basket, Czeslaw's knife – and Pog's red stone. And he's asleep. So why are we rowing?'

Mee said, 'Yes, yes! Why aren't we – ?' Without wasting more words, she began filling the empty tins with black stones. Train wound lashings of the white line round them, leaving plenty of line free. 'Multi-cylinder engine,' he joked, grimly.

'But we've only got one red stone!'

'We'll break the stone and use each piece.'

'But you don't know that it will work if it's broken!'

'Well, we'll just have to find out. It's not powerful enough on its own.'

'All right – how do we break it?'

Train took the red stone, put it in the palm of his hand and started hitting it with the tin opener blade of Czeslaw's knife. He hit it until his hand hurt. 'It won't break!' he said, hollowly.

'It *got* to break! Try these!' She handed him a pair of pliers from the little locker. Train put the stone between the jaws and squeezed till his face was scarlet. 'It's no good.'

Mee said 'You squeeze, I'll hammer with the knife. That must work!'

It didn't work.

Train said, 'We've just *got* to break the thing.' He put the stone back in the jaws of the pliers and snatched the knife from Mee. Squeezing as hard as he could with his left hand, he gave a trial tap with the knife in his right . . .

. . . And the stone fell into a dozen pieces, which rattled to the bottom in the wastepaper basket and settled there, twinkling demurely.

'Well, I'll be – ' said Train, and started to laugh. Mee said, 'Let's find out if the red stone works now it's broken.' They filled a tomato soup tin with black pebbles and added a chip of red. The tin jumped and pulled. They looked at each other and smiled.

'We'll make sort of rockets', Train said, 'with the oars for sticks.'

Without another word they started work. They filled tins with black stones, plugged them in place with a twist of torn-off blanket, and lashed the tins to the blades of the oars. They tied some rope across the boat from one oar handle to the other to make a harness for their backs. The rockets pointed ahead of the dinghy, in a V.

'All right,' said Train, 'Let's load. Ready?'

'Ready. We'll both do the same things at the same time, OK?'

Both at once, they partly removed the blanket plugs in a tin; put in a piece of red pebble; replaced the plug. Immediately the 'rockets' shifted – jerked forward – pulled the ropes tight against their backs.

'Listen to that!' said Train. There was a chuckling, bubbling noise; the dinghy was moving, her bows thrusting against the waves.

'More loading?' said Mee, holding up another fragment of red pebble.

'OK. Both together again.'

Two more tins received two more fragments of red pebble. Now the dinghy leaped forward, buffeting the waves.

'Look at that!' said Train, his voice awed. 'Look behind you!'

Mee looked back. Behind them there was a smooth path with frilled white edges. 'Our wake! We must be doing seven or eight knots!' she said. The rope bit into their backs. Spray from the bows wetted their foreheads and cheeks.

Train checked their course by the compass and corrected it with the fin of the outboard motor, which he used as a rudder. He had the handle of the motor fairly far over but the wake still curved. He said, 'We're pulling to the left all the time . . . Look at the wake.'

She looked back – sure enough, the wake was still curved, despite the pull of the rudder. She said, 'I'll just shift my oar a bit, we can straighten out the pull that way – '

And then she froze. The last flat rays of the sun showed a knife-sharp horizon where sea met sky. But this clean line was interrupted by a black silhouette.

'The submarine!' she said. 'Look, Train! They're after us!'

*

Panic-stricken, they loaded and mounted the third

pair of tins and immediately wished they hadn't. The pull was enormous. To meet it, they had to lock their knees so that their legs made straight lines. Their feet were forced deep in the rubbery roll of the bows. The rope at their backs bit into their flesh.

The dinghy leapt ahead, almost planing on the waves. It was going like a speedboat: but it was going in a big circle and the little fin of the outboard motor could not straighten the course.

Mee shouted, 'We've got to do something, we've got to straighten out or we'll turn right round and meet them!'

There were sheets of spray. Pog woke up. He said, 'It's all WET, make it stop!' Train grabbed him and swung him over his shoulder so that Pog lay behind him, protected from the worst of the spray. Pog said, 'It's *still* all wet, *I'm* all wet!' but Train had others things to worry about. Mee was in trouble with her oar. She was pulling frantically at it, trying to swing the front of her 'rocket' further outwards, but it would not shift. Then suddenly it shifted too much and a whole loop of cord freed itself; the shaft of the oar darted forward like a javelin; then the taper of the shaft filled the loops and jammed in them; and the dinghy was hurtling along in a straight line, the newly angled 'rockets' pulling equally.

The dinghy said 'BLUT... er-blat, BLUT... BLUT BLUT... er-blat' as it plunged through the waves. It seemed to have a thick, clumsy, dim spirit of its own, urging it to go faster and faster – make more spray – batter down more waves with its blunt rubber nose. Pog shouted 'TOO WET!' and pounded against Train's back with his fists. Everything was mad and Train wanted to laugh.

Pog's voice stirred Mee. She leaned over and pulled the child's blankets around him and smiled shakily at him. Above the noise of the boat and the rhythmic splatter of spray, she shouted, 'The sub! It's still behind us! Right behind us!'

Train looked back. Mee was right. He said, 'Perhaps they haven't seen us. They didn't see us last time!'

She said 'They must have seen us. Can't we go faster?'

He said, 'You must be joking! . . . Any faster and we'll take off!'

The sky got darker. The submarine got bigger.

Pog said 'Take off. Oh yes.'

*

And then the submarine was alongside them, black and wet and hugely efficient. There were little human heads – but not Czeslaw's – black against the darkening sky, clustered in the conning tower. The conning tower was so high that Train and Mee could not recognize the heads.

The conning tower spoke. It cleared its metallic throat and bellowed, 'You kids! Stop that dinghy immediately! Stop it and we'll come and get you!'

'Arthur Sonning!' Mee said. Train said, 'Couldn't stop if we wanted to!' and laughed. Once he started laughing, he couldn't stop. Mee began to giggle chokingly.

'If you don't stop, we'll run you down!' thundered the conning tower's brazen voice. 'You hear me? We'll run you down!' But Train and Mee were weak with hysterical laughter and the dinghy was still rushing ahead, *B L U T . . . er-blat*, sometimes level with the conning tower, sometimes ahead, sometimes behind, a crazy clockwork mouse beside an enormous trumpeting elephant. 'Run us down . . . !' Train choked. 'Run us down! They think they can run us down! Oh, Lord!' And he laughed so much that his stomach and ribs hurt. Yet all the time, another part of his brain was watching him, and thinking, and planning.

The conning tower seemed to rise still higher into the sky, blacking out the light. Mee and Train stopped laughing to watch. They saw the rounded flanks of the ship emerge, water pouring off them. Great jets of water vapour spurted from somewhere and the water boiled as the submarine rose.

The dinghy went mad in the turbulence. It corkscrewed, wobbled, plunged – and charged the submarine! 'We'll run *you* down!' Train yelled, and the waves of laughter seized him again. The other part of his mind said, 'This is the end, you've had it now.' But the clown in him yelled with helpless mirth as the dinghy struck the submarine with a solemn *Boompf!*, tried to climb the sloping flanks; hung at a crazy angle half in and half out of the water – and then, rescued by a wave, slipped off, spun 180° and accelerated away, completely unharmed.

'Come back here!' yelled the conning tower's and Arthur's voice, sounding surprised and indignant. But already that voice was a hundred yards away. The dinghy was earnestly gathering speed and re-establishing its old pattern. *BLUT . . . er-blat, BLUT . . . er-blat, BLUTBLUT . . . er-blat*.

Mee and Train looked back at the dark shape in the dark sky. The shape was turning, very slowly: the huge fin of the conning tower narrowed, narrowed still more. Mee said, 'They're pointing her at us. Do you think – ?'

Train said, 'I wouldn't be surprised if they run us down. What else can they do?'

'But would Czeslaw let them? He can't be that bad – '

'Who says Czeslaw is still in control? Perhaps the Captain's taken over and Czeslaw's in irons or whatever it is. If that's happened, the best thing they could do is to run us down!'

There was a mild *Zick* in the water, very close. Arthur's voice, a long way away, called, 'That was a rifle bullet. Stop the dinghy or you'll be shot. Or run down. Take your choice. Stop the dinghy NOW!'

Mee said, 'I suppose we'll have to. There's Pog . . . he's crying, aren't you Pog? Poor old Pog, I'll cuddle you.'

Pog said, 'It's too wet here. Please take off. You said "take off", I heard you. Why don't you?' He made aeroplane noises and began to whimper.

Mee and Train looked at each other over his head.

Mee said, 'Why don't we?'

Train said, 'Yes, why don't we? It's all that's left.'

She said, 'It wouldn't work. Would it?'

'No. And what we're doing now won't work either. So?'

Pog said 'Wet!' disgustedly. Another bullet went *Zick*.

'Come on,' Mee said, 'Let's not be wet!'

'OK.' They began unloading the tins of the 'rockets' one by one, flinging the stones into the stainless steel bowl having first picked out the red-stone fragments. Train put these in a pocket. The dinghy slowed.

'Now what?'

Train said, 'Let's get all the black pebbles together in two containers: this wastepaper basket and the steel basin. They've both got lips. Can you tie a rope really tightly round each of them? I'll reload the tins.'

Mee said. 'We'll want the oars – ' and there was another *Zick*, then another, both some yards away. Arthur's amplified tough-guy voice called, 'Right, you kids! Last chance! Stop or we shoot! Or run you down! Got it?' Then, not in his tough-guy voice, Mee and Train heard him say, 'Hell, where are they?'

Mee said, 'They've lost us! They can't see us any more!'

'Hey, you're right! No "rockets", no wake, no nothing! Look, we've really got a chance! I'm going to lash this to the outboard motor while you lash the other one to the ring up front . . .'

Mee said, 'It's not going to work. It can't.' Train said, 'It might. We've got the wastepaper basket lifting the front and the steel basin lifting the stern. And I've rigged lines to tilt the basket and the basin - to balance out the lift up and the pull along. As long as we put the power in bit by bit, so we don't get tipped out - '

'We can tie ourselves in. Pog, anyway. And we can use the oars to keep some sort of balance, can't we?'

'It's worth a try. Anything's worth a try. If only there was some light!'

At that moment there was light. The submarine's searchlights came on.

'Pointing in the wrong direction!' said Train. 'So they really have lost sight of us!'

'But they'll pick us up,' said Mee. Both of them whispered, as if the searching lights made it possible for the submarine to hear them.

'I don't think so, we're so low in the water. And we're not showing anything shiny, are we?'

'The outboard might show up, it's white - '

'You're right!' Train scuttled aft, struggled with the outboard's clamps and at last unshipped it and let it sink. 'Back to work!'

'Number one,' breathed Mee. While Train held

the blanket-draped stainless steel basin over his head, Mee carefully placed the first, unloaded tin full of black pebbles against the underside of the basin. She tilted the tin just enough to accept a piece of red pebble – fed the piece in – and heard a *Tang!* as all the pebbles slammed upwards against the basin.

'Great!' breathed Train. 'Pulling like mad! Do another tin!'

She did another. Now the basin pulled its restraining lines taut as cello strings: and the line of the pull was straight up, into the sky.

'Let's do the basket,' said Train. 'Keep it all balanced. First one, then the other.'

'Right.' Soon the wastepaper basket, loaded like the basin with tins of Antigrav, pulled its lines taut.

'Look!' said Mee, pointing at the centre of the dinghy's inflated roll. In each, there was a crease. The pull at the bows and stern was so strong that it was trying to fold the boat in two. Mee said, 'Tie some tins to the rowlocks!'

They did this and the crease disappeared. Now, the dinghy was being pulled in four places: bows, stern and both sides.

'More?' said Mee. Her eyes gleamed in the reflected light of the submarine's searchlights, which roved methodically over the waters. 'More!' said Train.

Still a long way away, Arthur's voice called 'This is it! Last chance! You have one minute!'

'Poor old Arthur!' said Train, and added more Antigrav to the basket. The front lifted like a shark's snout and stood out of the water. Deep creases formed amidships. 'She's trying to lift!' said Mee. And then, in a very different voice, she said, 'And we're going to run out of tins!'

'We don't need tins,' said Train. 'Just packages of black stones wrapped in bits of blanket. Like this . . .'

The stern of the boat lifted too.

Arthur's voice said, 'The minute is now up. One of you stand up. One of you stand up in the dinghy and wave your arms. We are coming to get you.'

'Ha, ha,' said Train. But Mee said, 'His voice was much closer that time!'

'More for the rowlocks to keep the sides up. Quick. OK? Here's the piece of red pebble, going in . . . *now*! Right. And the other . . . *now*!'

Then there was a sick, empty feeling. The dinghy, almost weightless, spun uneasily, trying to find its balance in three dimensions and failing. Pog said, 'I don't like that!' and whimpered. Mee said, 'Quick! The searchlights! They've found us!'

Train hissed 'This time!' and, eyes glaring, said, 'One more where you're sitting! Another package!' She scrabbled with blankets and black stones and a piece of cord – made a parcel – and showed Train the piece of red stone, ready to add to the package. 'Now?' she said.

'Are you roped to the dinghy? Is Pog?'

'Yes! Hurry, the searchlights! – they'll be coming for us! – '

'Right! Put it in! Put it in!'

She thrust the package up among the tins in the

stainless steel basin - fumbled the red stone in among the black - and had just time to shout 'No, it's all wrong!' as, with a sickening, twisting lurch, the dinghy almost completely folded in the middle, sucked at the water, swung wildly, and rose from the surface of the sea, into the sky.

On the submarine, the searchlights held on a grey, untidy, folded bolster hanging by threads from metal containers. The bolster dripped water and shed blankets as it limped from the sea up into the night sky. A sailor with a rifle crossed himself instead of shooting. Arthur Sonning in a hoarse monotone, said, 'I don't believe it, I don't believe it, I don't believe it . . .' The Captain swore at the sailor with the rifle, seized the weapon and furiously emptied the magazine at the grey lopsided thing. He never hit it.

It kept rising, still spinning slowly, still spilling drops of water and little objects that made small splashes as they hit the water.

It rose until the searchlights no longer lit it clearly: until the light of the moon, whose gravity pulled the crazy craft towards it, cast a cold, pale glow on three heads huddled together.

'Take off,' said Pog. 'Not wet: cold.'

*

It was Train who said it, but they had both been thinking of it: 'We'll never in a thousand years find the island.'

The dinghy was contorting itself into even worse shape . . . At first it had been like a fat sandwich with its ends folded upward. Mee, Train and Pog were squeezed in the middle. Now, something was wrong with the pull either end. The fat sandwich was trying to twist one half against the other. If it succeeded, the people inside would be squeezed out.

Mee pulled at the cords holding the wastepaper basket while Train yanked at those attached to the basin. 'Hold on to my leg, Pog!' Train shouted as the dinghy heaved and squeezed rubberily, changing its shape as the pull of the cords changed. Pog clasped his arms round Train's leg and said, 'Flying boat!'

They got the dinghy in a better trim. 'How high are we?' Mee asked. There was still light enough to see, dimly, each other's faces and the ocean below. It looked a long way away . . . 'Too high!' Train said and struggled with an oar. Pog said, 'Up? We're still going up . . . ?'

'Either up,' Mee told him, 'or down. That's definite.'

'Good,' Pog said, uncertainly. Time passed.

Train said, 'At least there's one good thing. We still know where west is.' He pointed to the dim glow of light on the horizon where the sun had set. Mee said, 'Another good thing: the moon's right, too. It's over to the west. It's pulling us in the right direction. We're lucky, aren't we, Pog?'

'Lucky,' Pog said miserably. 'Oh, yes.' He was very tired. The flight was already taking too long. Mee and Train hunched and shivered. The sky turned black.

Mee said, 'We'll play cops and robbers. Come on, Pog, I'll tie you up!' Fumbling in the dark, they tied his wrists together with a piece torn from Mee's shirt; then tied this with four separate loops of strong cord to the D-shaped rubber loops that formed the dinghy's rowlocks. By the time they had finished, he was asleep. 'Well,' Train said, 'He can't fall out now, whatever we do. But we can, so let's go carefully.' As he spoke, his knees felt a mild, muffled shock and Mee screamed.

'The sea!' she yelled. 'We're down! We've hit the sea!'

More muffled shocks and buffets: the dinghy was skimming the waves, sometimes hitting them. Train said, 'Hell, hell, what do we do! What do we *do*! – ' and began pulling at the cords, 'The knife!' he shouted. 'I'll cut the cords! – '

'No, don't! Wait! Don't cut anything!'

'But we'll be pitched out!'

'No, wait. Think!' She grabbed Pog – he was still more than half asleep – and said '*Think*!' Her face was a grey-white blob in the darkness. The dinghy went *Boompf!* again, not heavily, as it hit another wave top.

Mee said, 'Does it matter if we come down and stay down? Does it? We could always get up again if we had to . . .'

The dinghy hit a wave heavily – *Boompf!* – and Pog whimpered in his half-sleep. 'If we hit much harder than that – .' Train began, but stopped.

Mee said, 'How far are we from the sub? Can they catch us, do you think? How long were we up?

Are they so close that they'll see us when it's dawn?'

Train said, 'I don't know! How can I tell? Look, why should they want to catch us?'

'To keep us quiet,' Mee said. 'Czeslaw's not in charge any more! They'd kill us to keep us quiet, don't you see? Just to stop the Antigrav story getting out, and the kidnapping, and Leo and Arthur being involved and everything. They might even kill people on Tarantay Ear!'

The dinghy hit two waves hard and there was spray everywhere. The dinghy did not rise. Pog woke up and said, 'I want my pot, I need my pot –' But then he was asleep again.

Train said, 'Look. You're right. We've got to get to the island – or somewhere, anywhere – fast. We've got to fly and warn people. We've got to take off again. But first we've got to know if we're travelling west. I mean, actually *moving*, not just going up or coming down. Lean over the sides. Put your hand in the water.'

They leaned over the sides and felt the water. The water moved, pressing against their hands. 'We're moving,' Mee said. 'We're being pulled along. Definitely. Yes?'

'Yes.'

'Now what?'

'Now we point the wastepaper basket and the basin less at the moon and more to the sky, and we ought to go up again.'

They began undoing and retying knots. The

dinghy went *Boompf*. It was difficult working in the dark and every *boompf* made their hearts leap and their hands clutch for support. They worked on until Train said, 'Notice something?'

'What?'

'No more bumps. We're clear of the water. We're flying again! If only we knew how fast we're rising and how high up we are . . .'

Mee said, 'Give me all the rest of the cord.' She began doing things with her arms. Train could only half-see her movements, they looked like deep-breathing exercises.

She said, 'About 150 feet. That's the length of my outspread arms, say five feet, times thirty. I've got a line 150 feet long.'

'Brilliant!' Train said. 'Now we tie something to the end of the line and chuck it overboard. Right?'

'Tin can,' Mee replied. 'The can will catch in the water.'

She tied on the can, threw it over the side and started paying out the line, counting each arm's-width length. When she got to seventy-five, she stopped and gave the line to Train. 'Feel it!' she said. He held the line and felt the jerks and tugs of the can bucking against the water. After a time, the tugging stopped. 'We're still rising,' he said. 'The can's out of the water now. But it was there for quite a long time, so we can't be rising too fast. Clever old you.' He gave her back the line.

She crouched over it, feeling its pull. 'We're really travelling! The tin's pulling like mad. It's like holding a kite, only the wrong way round. You feel.'

He took the line. It pulled hard enough to cut into the palm of his hand. Then suddenly the pull was gone, the can had been lifted out of the water by the ascent of the dinghy . . .

And there was a sound, a noise.

Da-rang! Tang, tang-tang! . . . tang!

Then silence.

'Do you know what that was?' Train said at last. 'That wasn't water! That was our tin striking something solid. Land!'

*

But it was an hour later before they saw the lights. There were very few of them, widely scattered and some hundreds of feet below.

'Pull like mad!' Train said, and began tugging at the lines that held the downward edges of the wastepaper basket. Mee pulled the basin's lines. The dinghy swooped, accelerated and plunged down so fast that they had to let go and start again, more gently.

The lights were beneath them now. A single street, a curve of street lamps and one house – if it was a house – with lights in the window.

They pulled cords and let the dinghy swoop down again.

There was a big lake, you could see it pale and luminous in the moonlight. The water came up to meet them, slowly at first, then much too fast.

'Let go the lines!' Train shouted, and the lake hit them hard with a flat wet smack.

Pog woke up and said, 'My pot, I need it.'

Mee said, 'Just a minute longer, Pog. See over there, Train, where the light is?' They headed the dinghy for the light.

*

Ten minutes later, they were in the company of four London businessmen, come to Scotland for the fishing. The men were slow and sleepy at first, but then suddenly woke up and asked questions: too many questions. Mee and Train answered as best they could, but Pog kept saying, 'My pebble, Pog's pebble! They wanted it.' 'Who wanted it?' said one of the men. 'The man with no hair. In the submarine,' Pog said. 'We flew and they chased us.'

The man stared at Pog then directed round, questioning eyes at Mee and Train. Train nudged Mee, and shrugged. Mee said, 'He's only a little boy and he's very tired.'

In the end, one of the four men took them to the police station. 'Do we tell the police?' Mee whispered as they drove through the mountainous countryside, already beginning to glow with pale dawn light. 'Tell nobody nothing,' Train muttered.

The police station was a small stone house staffed by a sleepy black dog and an all-black bicycle outside; and a big ginger and red policeman inside. He did not ask them questions. He told them about his dog's way of catching Fush. As he talked, he made thick, sweet tea and the dog stared at them with sad, amber-coloured eyes. 'Fush?' thought Mee, 'What are Fush?' She was too polite and tired to ask. The answer came to her when she had drunk half her cup of tea. 'Fish!' she murmured, and her head fell forward. She slept, with the sleeping Pog as a prop and headrest, and dreamed of great silver fish with red pebbles for eyes.

When she woke properly, Pog was shouting, 'Heliclopter! Heliclopter!' in her ear, and she found herself in an Army helicopter, roaring and shaking. Train said, 'You've been asleep all this time!' She said, 'I know.' He said, 'That policeman, his dog catches fish!' She said, 'I know,' and fell asleep again.

Then her mother's arms were round her and Pog, and Train's father was staring at his son. They just stood, each with the same deep crease at the side of their mouths, staring at each other.

They were back again, back on Tarantay Ear.

*

When the explanations were finished, Train's father said, 'That man Czeslaw . . . I wonder what they'll do to him? And his wife?'

Pog said, 'We were in a submarine, oh yes.' Mee's mother, Peg, said, 'I don't think you'll see that submarine again. What do you think, Alan?'

'No, it's over and done with. They wanted Pog's

pebble. They didn't get it. What can they do now?'

'Invade this island,' Train said. 'Just use the submarine and – '

'I don't think so,' his father said. 'What excuse could they find for making an armed landing on British territory? Anyway, the Army's here.'

They all looked down at the group of soldiers near the sea. Some of the soldiers had already stripped to the waist: yet another hot day was beginning. The soldiers were unhurried. They knew what they were doing. The two guns the helicopter had dropped were already crouched between their fat rubber wheels, pointing out to sea. Now the soldiers were drinking tea and making signs to Pog. Pog glanced at his mother. She said, 'All right,' and he ran to the soldiers, falling down and picking himself up. Soon he was a General, riding a soldier's shoulders and inspecting the guns. They gave him a beret hat to wear. He made everyone salute him.

*

'The red pebble,' Train's father said, throwing it from one hand to another. They had stuck the pieces together again to please Pog. Mee shuddered, remembering Czeslaw. 'Please – don't do that,' she said.

'Well, what shall we do with it?' Train said.

'It's Pog's pebble,' Peg reminded them. But Alan said, 'Not really. It's the world's. So much power, for good or bad . . .'

Train said, 'That's what Czeslaw said, more or less. So much power. Too much power.'

'I'd like to simply throw it away,' Mee said. 'Throw it back in the sea.' They looked at each other, thinking it out.

Pog came roaring back, face scarlet and eyes alight. 'Tea in a mug!' he announced. 'Hot, oh yes! The soldiers did give it!' He saw the pebble and his face changed. 'My pebble,' he said. 'I need it.' He reached out his hand.

But Peg said, 'Pog, if you'll give us the pebble, we'll give you a great big enormous present. Anything you want.' She looked round at the others and said, 'Is that right?'

One by one, they nodded.

Pog said, 'Anything?'

'Anything at all, Pog. But you've got to give us the pebble.'

He said, 'Anything?'

Peg nodded. Pog stared at nothing, thinking hard. His lower lip stuck out. At last he said, 'Soldier-gun-on-wheels-with-real-bullets!' and stared at his mother, challengingly.

She said 'Done!' and shook hands with him. Alan Traynor got up and went to talk to the Officer in command of the troops.

The next helicopter to land included in its cargo a big cardboard box. Inside the box was a splendid toy Army gun on wheels. The gun was so big that it could fire ping-pong balls. The Officer presented it to Pog, who whispered, 'Oh, yes!' and saluted. The Officer saluted back. Pog placed the pebble in his mother's hand. She took it and said, 'Thank you, Pog.'

Train nudged Mee and pointed at the sticker on the cardboard box. It read '£5.35.'

'Good bargain, bad bargain?' he said. In Czeslaw's voice.

'Good bargain,' she replied.

*

When Pog, with one hand resting on the gun, was at last asleep, they all made their way down to the shore. Peg and Alan were arm in arm. Train carried Pog's pebble.

They stood under a blue-velvet moonlit sky by dark water and bright foam. Mee said, 'Who's going to do it?'

Train's father said, 'We'll skim stones. The winner does it.'

Peg's mother threw the first stone. It made one splash and that was all. 'She did it deliberately,' Mee said to herself, 'because she thinks it ought to be one of us. Train or me.'

Mee threw her stone. It hit, bounced, soared, and then made five white marks in the dark water. Train lied, 'Six. Not bad.'

Train's father threw his stone. Five.

Train threw. His stone hit the top of a wave, rocketed away and skittered over the water. You couldn't count the bounces. 'I make that four,' he said.

'No, it was seven! Eight! It went on and on, I saw it,' Mee said.

'How many bounces, Dad?' Train asked his father.

'Four,' his father lied, flatly. 'So it's up to you, Mee.'

Train handed her the red stone. 'I suddenly don't want to do it . . .' she said. 'It doesn't seem right.'

'Do it,' Train said in a low voice. 'Do it now.'

She sighed, stretched her arm far behind her, and threw.

They could not follow the flight of the stone. But they heard the distant sound as it struck the water and saw in their minds its slow, twisting, uncertain, fall to the depth where it would join thousands upon thousands of other stones and pebbles. And there it would lie forever.

Silently, they made their way back to where Pog lay, smiling in his sleep, with a hand resting on the Army gun.

Many months later . . .

Alan glared over the top of his spectacles and said, 'Who's been spreading marmalade on the newspaper?' He directed the glare at Train. 'I haven't even *looked* at the paper!' Train began, when Peg came in with more toast. She set it before her husband. They had been married for five months. To Train and Mee, it might have been five or fifteen years: the old days were half-forgotten, the new days were good.

'Marmalade?' Peg said. 'I'm sorry, it was me. I just sat there, with marmalade dripping from the spoon, when I read it – '

'Read what?'

'Page seven. The big photograph. Look at it.'

Alan did as he was told. One eyebrow went up. 'Train. Mee. Look. An old friend of yours.'

Train and Mee looked at the paper and saw Leo's face, topped with a fur hat, beaming at them from the page. Mee read out the headline:

DEFECTING SCIENTIST
SAYS 'NO REGRETS'

'No regrets . . .' Peg said. 'Not quite what he wrote in that letter to me.'

'Can I put this bit in the scrapbook, Mum?' Mee asked. She went to get the scrapbook, patting Alan on the head as she passed him. He growled, 'Hands off the bald spot.'

*

She came back with the scrapbook and turned first, as always, to the newspaper photograph – taken on the island – of Pog with his Army Gun. The photograph was exactly right. It showed Pog with legs apart, stomach out, plump arms locked tightly round his gun. His face was solemn, filled with a pleasure too deep for smiles. Mee smiled for him.

*

Her smile faded as she turned the page. Myra, in an airport lounge, with a hand up to try to hide her face. GIRL SCIENTIST SEEKS ASYLUM. Myra had escaped (but how?) from the country to which the submarine had taken her. Here she was in Israel (why?) being turned away by the authorities. What would she do next? Where would she go? There were several newspaper stories, all short, about Myra. Would there ever be a final story, with a happy ending?

Train was looking over her shoulder. 'She was one of the Baddies,' he said, without conviction. Mee said, 'Yes, I suppose so. But I keep thinking of her and wishing she could have . . .'

'Started from somewhere else?' said Train.

'Yes, that's it. Everything was impossible for her, what could she do?'

Train shook his head and said, 'Turn over.'

*

Arthur Sonning. Another photograph taken in a foreign airport lounge. Arthur's face was frozen by flashlight in a triumphant grin: 'Look at me! I'm here! I've made it!' the picture seemed to say.

But around him stood the men – the solid, patient, flat-faced, thick-bodied officials. Their eyes were fixed on Arthur. Their faces were unsmiling.

'You poor sap!' Train said to Arthur's photograph, and turned the page.

*

'Here it is, Mum. Your letter from Leo,' Train said. Peg took the letter from the scrapbook and frowned at the bold, flowing writing. 'A waste of paper,' she said. But Alan said, 'No, read it out. It's a classic of its kind.' Peg started reading:

Peg, dear –
I'm in two minds about writing to you – and not at all certain that what I write will ever reach you! But our relationship is one link in my life's chain that can never be broken –

With gloomy pleasure, Alan murmured, 'I like that. Poetic.'

– can never be broken. You see, Peg, although everyone here has been overwhelmingly kind, I can't forget the debt I owe the land of my birth –

'Better still,' Alan said, trying not to smile.

Sometimes, I admit, I feel very much alone, even in the hustle of the TV studios or chatting about matters scientific with my many new friends –

'*Chatting,*' said Alan, appreciatively. 'He hasn't got a word of their language, but he chats. About matters scientific. I wish I could be there . . .'

Nothing in this life is ever fixed, is it? And if, at some time in the future, it happens that I change course –

'Become a double traitor,' Alan said.

– a word from you in the right quarters could be

invaluable. You know what I mean by the right quarters – you've still got my address book, haven't you? – so if you could possibly –

'In other words,' Alan said, 'He wants you to keep his seat warm over here!'

'But could he ever come back?' Train said. 'Would they let him out?'

'Not a chance in a million. He's there and he'll stay there. Sooner or later they'll get bored with him. And then – '

'Then what?' Train asked.

'Well, you know how they've handled Czeslaw,' Alan said.

Peg turned the scrapbook's pages.

*

OLD SOLDIERS NEVER DIE
THEY ONLY FADE AWAY

announced the headline. There were two big pictures of Czeslaw from the front page of a newspaper. One showed him as they all knew him – massive, masterful, totally bald: the other, as a young, bushy-haired, fierce-eyed Army Officer of the Second World War. THE TIGER OF THE FROZEN PLAINS, said the old headlines.

The present-day story ran, 'The continuing mystery surrounding the disappearance of Czeslaw has been solved in part by a recent reference to the soldier-scientist's "hospitalization", said to be the result of "a serious heart disease" – '

'– Leading to "heart failure" any moment now,' said Alan. 'Poor devil.'

'They'll have to give him a hero's funeral, like it or not,' Mee said.

'Because he was a war hero, you mean?' said Train.

'And after,' Mee said. 'Anyhow, he was a hero as far as *we* were concerned. Good, bad . . . Do you remember him saying that? Working out what he ought to do about us, and Pog's pebble?'

'And the world,' said Train. 'A world hero . . .'

*

Pog ran in from the garden. In his left hand he held two worms, already forgotten. For in his right hand, he held a pebble. 'Look!' he said, 'Pebble again! Red! Mine!'

Mee snatched it from him and stared at it, white-faced. Then she smiled and let him take his pebble back. 'Black stones now,' Pog said. 'Then up in the air. Oh yes!' He trotted off.

'It wasn't – ?' Train said.

'No. Of course not. Just a little red pebble.'

Pog came back. 'It *will* fly,' he began, uncertainly.

'Well, that will be marvellous!' Mee said.

'But s'pose it doesn't?' Pog said.

'That will be better still,' Mee said, under her breath.

ABOUT THE AUTHOR

Nicholas Fisk wrote his first complete book when he was nine. It was about a baby fox and was very sentimental. He first earned money from writing when he was sixteen. When he finished his R.A.F. service, he became an actor, jazz musician, illustrator and writer for all kinds of publications.

His interests include snorkelling, cars, old microscopes, building a swimming pool, photography (he has published a book on the subject), and a dozen other things. He finds that writing is hard and lonely work, but enjoys writing 'science fiction' (meaning stories about extraordinary things that *could* happen) for young people. They seem to understand how fast the world is changing, whereas most older people do not.

His other books in Puffins are: *Grinny*, *Space Hostages*, *Time Trap*, *Trillions* and *Wheelie in the Stars*.

Heard about the Puffin Club?

... it's a way of finding out more about Puffin books and authors, of winning prizes (in competitions), sharing jokes, a secret code, and perhaps seeing your name in print! When you join you get a copy of our magazine, *Puffin Post*, sent to you four times a year, a badge and a membership book.

For details of subscription and an application form, send a stamped addressed envelope to:

The Puffin Club Dept A
Penguin Books Limited
Bath Road
Harmondsworth
Middlesex UB7 0DA

and if you live in Australia, please write to:

The Australian Puffin Club
Penguin Books Australia Limited
P.O. Box 257
Ringwood
Victoria 3134